Easy Bake Covenant

Jessica Gleason

Cover Design, Cover Art by Maciej Kamuda

E-Book Edition ISBN: 978-1-967519-08-8

Paperback Edition ISBN: 978-1-967519-09-5

Hardback Edition ISBN: 978-1-967519-25-5

Burial Books LLC
4000 Eagle Point Corporate Drive, Suite 303
Birmingham, AL 35242
www.burialbooks.com

Also by Jessica Gleason

Novellas
The Fabulous Miss Fortune
The Dangerous Miss Ventriloquist
Playing Hooky
Madison Murphy
Damned Before Daylight

Poetry Collection
Sundown on this Town

Prologue

Evil isn't straightforward. It doesn't invite you to sit down for tea, laying out the terms of its deception. No. Evil lulls you into a false sense of security. It appeals to your desires, needs, and wants. It twists your weaknesses and uses them against you with a sly grin on its face. You might ask yourself how people fall into evil's grasp time and time again. Surely, the red Devil and his grand horns are a shining beacon in the darkness, screaming out a warning to stay away. But it's never that simple, is it?

You can fall into evil's grasp without even realizing it and then one day the Devil comes to collect his due. Be cautious. Be wary. If it seems strange, walk—no, run away. If it sounds too good to be true, it is. Most importantly, do not agree to or sign anything unless you've read the fine print. That is key. Evading evil and its soulless hunger can be a full-time job if you're not careful.

Then again, there is beauty in the dark if only you look at it the right way.

Chapter 1

Laura sat on the steps outside her mother's quilting shop, stomping on ants and daydreaming, when she was interrupted by a noisy commotion from across the road.

"Get away from my house!" shouted a filthy wisp of a woman each time passersby strayed near her makeshift home. Her wild mannerisms were erratic and jerky as she jangled about like a possessed marionette.

"If you step any closer to my house, I'll bite you," she cried, her shrill voice carrying on the wind all the way to the other side of the street. "Chomp! Chomp! Right down to the bone." The woman brandished her rotting teeth in a sideways grin, letting spittle fall from the open corner of her puckered mouth. "And you'll run away screaming while I lick your warm blood from my lips."

They lived in a small Midwestern town where this sort of thing was an anomaly, and no one was well-equipped for how to act in a situation such as this. Folks sidestepped the strange woman quickly, various horrified expressions scrawling across their innocent faces. Not daring to make eye contact or respond, they shuffled along, attempting to evade the terrifying woman's advances. She was the kind of woman most folks didn't really see, per se; a woman who wasn't given the dignity of acknowledgment unless she made a spectacle of herself. And it seemed this particular woman was adept at spectacle making.

Greasy strands of white hair hung, shielding the shrieking woman's face, as she bustled about, rearranging her belongings. Digging deep into trash bags, she tossed empty cartons and ratty toys out onto the cobblestone street behind her. Occasionally, she'd dart into and back out of the tent, bringing with her some shiny treasure or peculiar totem. The woman felt off-putting, but her vivid blue eyes were wild and alive, reflecting brightly in the warm sunlight of early afternoon.

Laura, in her favorite overalls, watched in awe, standing safely in the alcove of What's Sewing On as the bizarre scene unfolded in front of her. Though young, she was more curious than afraid of the odd behavior. The woman's weathered skin and flowing black clothing were much different from the dumpy blue Talbots suits her mother loved to wear to work, and Laura found her aggressive nature somewhat alluring.

What an interesting weirdo.

"You there, girl," the woman called from across the town's cobblestone road. "Girlie! Yes, you, over there."

Laura jolted back to reality, ashamed to have been caught staring and a little startled by the woman's sudden attention. She looked to her left and then to her right, spotting no one save a large man struggling to unlock the door to his nearby insurance office, before looking back at the peculiar woman and responding, "Me?"

"Yes, you, little brown-haired girl. Are there any other girls sitting around out here? Will you just come over here?" she asked, using her knobby pointer finger to summon Laura from across the road.

Laura, putting on what she hoped was her most confident face, yelled back across the road with her head held high, "I'm not supposed to talk to strangers. Sorry."

A sly, less intimidating grin broke out across the woman's face as she laughed at the child's ridiculous response. "Well, you've already broken that rule, haven't you? We're talking right now."

Laura percolated for a moment; the odd woman certainly had a point. "Um... I guess so. Dang."

"And has anything bad happened to you?"

"Well, no."

"Then come over here. I haven't got all day, you know."

Trying to come up with a reason to stay in the safe shade under the banner of her mother's store, she let out a lame, "I'm not supposed to leave the property," and held up her left arm in a half-shrug.

A hint of annoyance crossed the bedraggled woman's face, but she kept up her friendly demeanor. "Well, I won't tell if you don't. It's only a few extra steps, right?"

Laura sat in quiet contemplation while the woman's eyes bored into her. "Okay, as long as my mom doesn't see," she replied before getting up and tiptoeing across the road.

This is a bad idea.

Since it was midday, and her mother would clearly see her if she looked out the window, Laura thought sneaking would be best.

"You're a strange girl, aren't you?" The woman peered at her, eyebrow raised, with curiosity.

Up close, the woman looked much older. Her face sagged with the memories of her younger and untamed years. Her fingers were crooked and calloused, and she was so thin that Laura wondered how she was supporting her big head without breaking in half. "If I'm strange, then what are you?"

"Brave words, girlie. Brave words." The woman's humored expression betrayed her more stern response.

Laura crossed her arms and eyed the woman suspiciously. "Well, what am I doing over here? Are you going to kidnap me? My mom would probably notice if you did!"

Taken aback, the woman replied, "Why would you ask me that?"

"Well, you don't seem very nice," Laura responded, the words flying from her mouth before she had the chance to think them through. Her mouth hung open in shock at the realization of her rude blurting. Still, she didn't fear the woman in front of her.

"I nicely asked you to come over here, didn't I?"

She considered the woman's question before replying, "I suppose, but you were yelling at all those people before, and it didn't sound very friendly at all."

"Hmmmm..." the woman began. "That's what happens when someone gets too close to my house. Do you like people getting close to your house? Huh, girlie?"

"I don't know."

"Well, someday you will."

"Okay, but you still didn't answer my question. Why am I here? I shouldn't stay over here long. My mom will yell at me." Laura shuffled back and forth nervously, knowing she was tempting fate and that her mother would ground her if she caught her talking to a strange lady on the other side of the road. She was certainly old enough to cross the street on her own, but her mother worried something might happen to her in town if she left the safety of the shop. As far as towns went, this one seemed safe enough to Laura, but she wasn't an expert in town crime.

The woman disappeared into her makeshift home and rattled around a bit, clinking together what sounded like pots and pans or, perhaps, cymbals from a drum set, before coming out with a small white trash bag trailing behind her. She walked over to Laura and plopped the bag onto the sidewalk in front of her.

"Um... What's this?"

"A present."

"Why would you give me a present? What the heck is in here?"

The woman leaned in with a conspiratorial look on her face, her hot breath wreaking of old cheese, before almost whispering her reply, "I've been waiting for the right little girl to give this to. It's very special to me, but I think it's time to pass it on."

Laura peeked into the bag and looked back at the woman questioningly. "What's this?"

She sighed. "You kids. That's a bag of fun. Haven't you ever seen an Easy-Bake Oven before?"

Laura had no idea what an Easy-Bake Oven was, but did her best to save face. "Maybe? What's it for?"

"Well, you bake with it, obviously. Don't children know anything these days? These were popular when I was a little girl. I've even added some unopened cake mixes too, chocolatey cakes. Don't all little girls love chocolate cake?" She paused, looking back at Laura with one eyebrow raised. "I'll take that as a yes. It's settled then. You'll accept the gift. Make sure to try each cake mix. You'll love it."

"Why would I need this? I've got a regular oven at home, and I don't think I should take food from a strange lady on a street corner," Laura retorted, not terribly interested in what the woman was offering.

"You're not. You're taking mixes that you can turn into food and a way to make that happen. That's not at all the same thing. This is no different than getting one at Goodwill, except you don't have to pay me. I'm giving this to you out of the kindness of my heart. And, besides, aren't we friends now?" She placed a hand across her heart and stared at Laura with those wild sapphire eyes.

Laura considered the woman's question. They weren't friends, no. But she was being cordial, neighborly even, in her odd way. "I guess so."

"Good. It's settled then. You'll be doing me a favor by taking some of this clutter away."

Biting her lip before responding, Laura weighed her options and decided there was no harm in accepting the gift. "Uh, okay."

"So, you'll take it?" the woman asked, scanning Laura's freckled face and waiting for a verbal confirmation.

"Yes."

"And you'll use it? Of your own free will and volition?"

"Uh...I guess...but that's a weird question to ask." Laura thought things were getting stranger as the seconds passed, and she felt the urge to bolt back to safety.

"Yes or no?" the woman demanded. "When someone asks you a question, you give a concrete answer."

"Yes then," Laura replied. "I'll use it. I promise."

"Excellent. Now, you scurry along home, little girl. I wouldn't want you to get into any trouble with that mother of yours." The woman's bony hand shot out, grasping Laura's arm a little too tightly just as she was stepping away. "But don't eat all those sweets at once, you hear me? It'll rot your teeth. One per day. Do you understand?"

Laura nodded. As the woman cackled to herself, Laura noticed the blackness inside her mouth, those cavity-ridden chompers a reminder to brush her teeth before bed. Laura went to pry the woman's fingers from her arm, spying three strange 9s scarred into the older woman's skin before quickly stepping backward, almost into the road.

"Um, thank you for this," Laura said, holding up the clunky trash bag.

"Use it well. You won't be sorry."

Won't be sorry? What an odd thing to say. Such a strange woman.

Chapter 2

DECIDING IT WAS BEST to head back to the comfort of her mom's store, she scurried across the road and into the well-lit shop. The welcome bells jangled as Laura came in, lugging the trash bag behind her. Her mother's shop had been nestled in the center of their sleepy town for her entire life and was, a little begrudgingly, a staple of her existence. She spent most after-school hours working on homework, reading, or doodling in the back room while her mother dealt with customers or worked on her newest quilting project. Quilting itself had never much appealed to Laura. She felt like it was for old ladies—not old like her mom, but the kind of old lady with deep puggle wrinkles and permed blue hair, the cheek-pinching kind. But her mother seemed to like it well enough, and her quilts were almost cool. Laura's mother had spent weeks on a full-size Transformers quilt when Laura was obsessed with robots in disguise. She still kept it folded in a chest at the end of her bed for especially cold nights.

Laura wasn't sure how a business like her mother's stood the test of time. The population of their little town was only about ten thousand people, and Laura assumed most of them did not quilt. They drank. The bars were always noisy and full. The restaurants seemed to fare well too. But the demand for quilting didn't seem large or urgent. Still, the little shop had been there for years, settled firmly between an expensive educational toy store that Laura hated and a used-book store which she loved.

As Laura entered the familiar space, she noticed an unnatural, breezy chill in the usually still air. Her breath puffed out in a cloud of air, and she watched as goosebumps popped up all the way down her gangly arms. It was too early in the year for air conditioning and too late for heat, so Laura was noticeably disturbed by the odd phenomena. As she shivered, she noticed the bright bolts of fabrics lining the shop's right wall, casting eerie shadows across the floor, claw-like shapes seeming to reach out from the darkened corners of the store. Feeling unsettled, she shook her head and dragged her bulky trash bag to the back of the shop where she usually stashed her things.

She dropped the bag into a somewhat cobwebby corner. In a flash, the store seemed normal again, quiet save the mechanical humming of her mother's favorite sewing machine. The temperature leveled out. The breeze stopped. The shadows dissipated. *Weird.* Laura hadn't put her finger on what exactly went wrong, but the blip had passed, and all was as it should be. She shook her head to clear the remaining odd feelings. Moments later, the peculiar shadows and shivering sensations were forgotten.

Looking up from her latest quilt, one made from old band t-shirts, Laura's mother eyed her suspiciously.

"What's in there?" she asked, gesturing to the bag Laura had listlessly plopped in the back office.

Laura shrugged in her mother's general direction, still feeling slightly guilty about the ordeal that led to her acquisition of said bag and not wanting to explain to her mother that she'd accepted a gift from the peculiar woman living in a tent across the street. "Nothing interesting," she mumbled, attempting to avoid her mother's probing gaze.

"Okay, you keep your secrets then." Her mother continued sewing for a moment before looking up abruptly and asking, "It's not a dead thing, is it?"

Laura clicked her tongue in annoyance. "Ew. No. Why would you ask me that?"

"Just being cautious. That's a warning sign, you know? Kids hauling around dead things. Taxidermy. All that stuff. I read about it in one of my thrillers." Her wide-eyed mother stared at her in earnest before tucking a stray strand of brown hair behind her ear and looking back down at her sewing.

"A warning sign for what?"

"Sociopaths. Psychopaths. And no daughter of mine is turning into a raccoon-dissecting would-be killer."

"Gross, Mom. I am not carrying dead things around in a trash bag. Who does that? You need to stop reading that kind of stuff. It'll rot your brain."

"It'll do what, now?" her mother asked, laughing at the odd turn of phrase.

"You heard me. That's what you say anytime you don't want me to watch or read something, isn't it?"

"I suppose so," she began. "We mothers worry. I know things have been hard since your father left. I just like to check in on my girl. I wasn't implying that you'd turn into a murderer, but I had to be sure." She looked up, winking at her daughter before looking back down again.

Laura rolled her eyes, but the effort was wasted, as her mother hadn't caught the gesture. "Ugh. I do not want to talk about any of this. Your jokes don't make it better. Can we not bring up Dad? I'm glad he's gone. End of story. He's a bad man."

Laura's mother nodded, a sad look on her face, before waving her daughter off and returning to work. "Just make sure you do your homework sometime before closing, okay? Thanks."

After grabbing a soda from the mini-fridge in the back room, Laura wandered the aisles aimlessly, her fingers mindlessly traipsing across the various-textured fabrics in the store, the memory of her unsettling entrance popping back into her head.

See, nothing unusual here. It's just cloth.

No spookies or scaries.

Ready to laugh, she thought herself silly for being afraid of some weird shadows. Though, as she paused to stare at a rack of buttons at the end of the aisle, something about the store's atmosphere still felt off to her. She pushed the prickly feeling to the back of her brain and went on with her work.

The rest of the day passed with no incidents. Laura paused several times to listen for odd creaks, hoping to catch mice or something that she could blame for the willies she'd experienced at the shop. No such rodents appeared. In fact, it was a slower day than usual. The quilt shop was mostly empty, save the occasional patron, and her mother was sewing away deep into the afternoon, humming hair metal ballads quietly to herself as she worked. Laura's thoughts drifted to an upcoming math test and a teacher who was the bane of her existence.

After finishing her math homework, Laura pulled out a worn copy of *Scary Stories to Tell in the Dark*. She'd outgrown the book a little, but found comfort in its familiarity. It was a classic, and she respected that. Reading it distracted her from her troubles and tempered her emotions. She didn't need the book anymore, having memorized every piece within its pages. But she loved the weight of it in her hands, the scent of its worn paper, and she secretly enjoyed all the dog-eared pages. She smiled, proud that she'd desecrated the book just a little, marked it as her own.

Laura alternated between sitting to read and reading while pacing the store until it was time to close up and head home. She waited while her mother finished counting the drawer and turning off the machines and lights for the day. As the afternoon wound into evening, Laura forgot about her morning encounter with the unhinged old woman and the strange gift she'd been given. She was just ready to go home and warm her belly with a plate of something savory and hearty.

"Alright, kiddo. Let's head out. Don't forget your...um... bag." Her mother lazily gestured to the crinkled trash bag in the back corner.

"Oh yeah," she replied, bounding to the back to grab her gift.

Looking at her with mock-stern eyes, her mother asked, "What's in it anyway? You never did say."

"Some little oven thing," Laura replied, rolling her eyes and dragging the bag along behind her.

"An oven thing? That bag is pretty small for an oven."

"Ugh. It's not a real oven, Mom. What would I even do with that? It's like a toy oven thing."

"Do you mean an Easy-Bake Oven?"

"Uh, I think so? Yeah, that's what it was called."

Her mother's face lit up, wistful and clearly reminiscing about her own younger years. "Where did you get one of those? I haven't seen one since I was a little girl."

"Long time ago then?" Laura asked, giggling through the question.

"Watch it, kid!"

"I'm just kidding, Mom. You know I love you and don't think you're old at all."

"Uh huh. So, where'd you get it?"

"I found it out by one of the dumpsters. It's probably a reject from the thrift store or something. It might not even work, but who am I to pass up free toys?" The lie effortlessly rolled off Laura's tongue, which both surprised and delighted her.

"What were you doing over by the dumpsters? You're supposed to stay in front of the store."

"I saw a weird toy sitting on the ground and needed to investigate."

Her mother looked skeptical, but if she was questioning things she didn't mention it. "Okay then. I had one of these when I was a little younger than you are now, and I absolutely loved it. I know you're older now, but I think you might still find some joy in it... Easy-Bake Oven," she mused. "I didn't even know they made them anymore. All you kids want digital toys and tablets. Who knew?"

While her mother was busy reminiscing about her own Easy-Bake childhood, seeming somewhat relieved that her daughter had taken an interest in something other than the iPad, the two hopped into the car and made their way home for the evening.

"I bet you'll have some fun with that thing. Before you know it, you'll want a Tamagotchi or something too." Her mother laughed, the jovial sound filling up the car's empty spaces.

"I don't know what that is, Mom."

"Of course not. You kids!" she said playfully. "Hey, Laura?"

"Yeah, Mom?"

Sensing some unease in her daughter, she reached out to place a supportive hand on her knee. "You're okay, right? We're okay?"

Laura hesitated, not wanting to answer her mother's loaded question. Was she okay? No. But none of that was her mother's fault. She didn't blame her for the sins of her father. But they'd been over that before. Perhaps her mother was sensing some lingering unease from earlier in the day. She offered her mom a weak smile. "We're good."

"As long as you're sure. You know I'm here to listen if you need me."

"Yeah, Mom, I know." Her words rang hollow. "I'm just tired, I think."

"Well, I've got a cure for that," she replied before cranking up Queen on the radio and belting out an off-key "Bohemian Rhapsody" the rest of the way home.

Laura feigned horror, but enjoyed seeing her mom have a little fun after a long day at the shop. Queen always helped her mom slough off some of her stress, and Laura thought her mother deserved at least that much. She was a good mom.

Chapter 3

ONCE HOME, LAURA RACED up the stairs of their comfortable Cape Cod, skipping every other one, tossed the bag into her room, and promptly forgot about it for the rest of the night. The pair, mother and daughter, enjoyed dinner before Laura sleepily climbed back up to her room. She fell backward onto the bed and drifted off to sleep without changing into pajamas, the day's stresses finally setting in. It was her mother who brought up the toy the next day.

Sleep still crusty in the corners of her eyes, Laura stretched, not ready to face the day. She rubbed one of her tired eyes and opened it, hissing at the bright sunlight peeking through the curtains. "Get out of here, sun. No one invited you. It's too early."

She looked down at the crumpled covers and sighed, noticing her still-clothed form. The sunlight rendered her too warm and too uncomfortable for sleep. Briefly, she wondered why cats loved being in the sunbeams so much. To her, it felt like misery.

However, the freedom of the weekend gave her the chance to be lazy, and she wanted to capitalize on the opportunity. Fall temps were in full bloom, and she knew moving away from the sunlight would render her more comfortable. She kicked off her pants, tossed them to the floor, and nestled back into her comfortable bed, shying away from the sliver of light on the right side of her bed. Closing her one eye again, Laura flopped onto her side, curled up into a ball, and attempted to go back to sleep.

As she was drifting off, a soft knock at her door interrupted her chance at sleep. "Ugh. What now?"

Laura's mother peeked her head inside, a warm smile on her lips. "Still in bed, sleepyhead?"

"Trying to be," Laura said, taking a pillow and playfully tossing it at her mother. "But an annoying parental figure is here to ruin that."

"Hey now. Calm yourself. I come in peace." She stepped into the room, holding her hands up in mock surrender. "I thought I might find you in here tinkering with that new toy of yours. Who doesn't want cake for breakfast?"

"It's too early to live, Mom. Who's thinking of breakfast at an unholy hour like this?" she asked dramatically before using the blankets to cover the bottom half of her face again.

"Laura, it's almost ten. Don't be ridiculous. I'm literally telling you to have cake for breakfast. Who turns that down?"

"I don't even know how to use that thing," she said, pulling the blankets up over her eyes to block out the light. "My brain is still asleep."

"Well, you plug it in, and you mix up the little mixes. Oh, do you have those? I guess maybe you don't. Do you want me to get you some?"

Laura sat up in bed with a harumph, giving up on sleep. "I think I have some. I'm pretty sure they come in the box," she replied, scratching her head and attempting to comb her fingers through her tangled brown hair.

"Was that box sealed? I don't like the idea of you eating trash food!"

"Uh...no. But the mixes are sealed. I'll check the expiration dates, I promise."

Her mother looked slightly uncomfortable with the idea, but continued. "Okay, well, you mix them up and pour them into the little cake tins, and then you shove it into the oven with a plastic arm thing. There's a light bulb inside. It'll cook your cakes or brownies or whatever. Then you eat it."

"That's all? It's just a light bulb in a box? It doesn't sound like much of a toy to me."

"What do you mean, that's all? It's fun. I used to beg my mom to let me play with mine. And trying new things might lead to surprising adventures or, perhaps, a hidden talent for baking!"

"Okay, Mom," she groaned. "Maybe I'll try it out today."

"Attagirl. Have fun! If you want more mixes, just let me know. I'll order some on Amazon. I'm sure they'll have them. They have everything. I bet you can make all sorts of things in that oven these days. Maybe I'll do some scrolling, for science!"

With that, her mother retreated, leaving her to her own devices. Laura stretched and searched the bed for her trusty copy of *More Scary Stories to Tell in the Dark*, the book she'd been reading when she fell asleep. The girl hadn't dropped it on her face this time, which was a positive change. Once she found it, sticking out from behind a stuffed animal, she placed it securely under her pillow for later and decided she would actually get out of bed.

She stood, stretching her limbs to the ceiling, and heard an audible pop as her shoulder cracked in the quiet room. "Ouch!" She shuffled forward a few steps and yawned while gazing longingly at her comfortable bed. Laura already wanted to crawl back in. The thought of hiding under the disheveled covers and sleeping until the afternoon appealed to her, but her brain didn't want to waste an entire day.

Stupid brain.

Not bothering to get dressed, she crossed her room in her long, wrinkled Kiss t-shirt, a hand-me-down from her mother, to investigate the Easy-Bake Oven. As she pulled it from the bag, she shivered once again but dismissed it as a typical fall morning chill. The oven looked slightly worn. The once-white plastic had yellowed around the edges, and the plug's prongs were slightly bent. However, it was indeed a tiny cooking toy, though it looked more like a weird microwave than an oven to Laura.

"Okay, we just plug it in." She shoved the plug into the socket, wiggling it a bit to get the bent prongs to fit correctly. Once she flipped the switch, the light bulb sprang to life, luminescent and a bit brighter than expected. "Check." Then, she reached into the bag to find mixes and bowls. There were precisely three packets of cake mix, all devil's food.

Well, that's a disappointment. No brownies? Red velvet?

She inspected everything, and the boxes and bags within the packages seemed sealed and new. So she felt they were safe enough to try out, even if there wasn't much variety. Part of her still didn't trust the odd woman who'd gifted her the relic, but she didn't want to be judgmental like all the people she'd seen glaring or muttering at the lady.

Maybe she was just a regular old lady who'd had a hard time of things.

Let's try this ancient toy out... I guess it's a good thing I like chocolate.

Laura spent the next several minutes running across the house to get water for her cake. She stirred the gloopy concoction, poured it into the small round tin that came with her Easy-Bake gift, and then stuffed the whole thing into the lit-up box using the strange plastic grabber tool. "I guess we just wait now."

The room was filled with a strange, though not unpleasant, aroma. It wasn't exactly the sweet cupcake scent that filled the house when her mother had the time to bake, but it did smell dessert-adjacent. After a few minutes, Laura popped her first cake out with the arm tool. Strangely, there was a thick red liquid oozing from the center of her creation, though nothing red had gone into the mix. "Hmmm... Maybe that's what it's supposed to look like?"

Laura waited for the curious confection to cool before using her fingers to pull pieces of her sticky brown and red cake from the small tin and shoving them into her mouth. "That's not half-bad," she said, savoring the rich chocolatey flavor. "But it was a lot of work for such a small snack."

Laura hadn't hated her Easy-Bake experience, but definitely felt like the toy had been made for someone a little younger than herself—eight or nine maybe, someone with a much smaller appetite. Once she finished, she headed down the stairs, intent on tossing her dirty pan into the sink. "Maybe that thing isn't so dumb after all. At least I got a snack out of the deal."

After her trip to the kitchen, she wandered into the living room, where her mother sat mindlessly watching television. As their eyes met, Laura couldn't help but feel a slight pang of guilt at her half-truth about the Easy-Bake Oven. Her mother, while a little dopey sometimes, looked at her with love and affection. Laura watched as she sat there in her worn gray sweats and her hair tied into a ponytail, all freckled and content. She liked that they had matching freckled faces, that she favored her mother and didn't have to look at her father's face in the mirror.

"Hey, Mom, I tried out the oven thing," she said. "I tossed the pan into the sink for you."

"Great, thanks. More dishes!"

"You're the one who told me to use that thing!"

The corners of her mother's mouth curled into a smile. "And how was it?"

"It was good, but it looked a little weird. I'm not sure baking is my thing."

Her mother nodded and reached out to pat her on the hand. "That's okay. We all have our thing. I'm glad you tried it out. New things are good for the soul."

Laura's tummy rumbled, and her mother laughed. "I think you should try a different mix next time. Maybe that one was expired."

"It wasn't! I looked!" Clutching her tummy, Laura nodded. "But you might be right. Something didn't agree with me. I think I'm going to go back upstairs and relax for a while or something. I'm not feeling great."

"Okay, honey. Yell if you need anything. I'll just be down here relaxing and catching up on my shows. I've got weeks of *SVU* to catch up on. Maybe put some pants on today, okay?"

"We'll see," Laura replied before tromping back up to her room, clutching her gurgling tummy.

She spent the morning and much of the afternoon scrolling through YouTube videos about cryptids while her stomach cramped. Her love of creepy things had evolved over time, and though she still liked revisiting Alvin Schwartz's stories, her current fascinations included Creepypastas and *Five Nights at Freddy's*.

"Laura, you wanna come down for something to eat?" her mother called from downstairs.

She glanced at the clock and scoffed at the bright red 5:30 PM staring back at her. Not having realized how late it had gotten, Laura groaned and powered her tablet off. Daylight was barely visible on the horizon, and night was taking hold. With a sigh and another tummy grumble, she headed downstairs for some food.

"Feeling any better?"

"I dunno, I've felt a little off since yesterday. It's probably nothing. What are we having?"

"I just made some mac and cheese. You want hot dogs in it?"

"Maybe not tonight," she said, thinking her stomach would protest about the hot dogs. "Is it cool if I just eat upstairs and read for a while?"

"Yeah, kiddo. It's the weekend. Have at it. You're sure you're okay? Do you want some Tums for that upset stomach? We can watch a movie or play a game or something to help distract you."

"No, that's okay. I think I'll be fine after a good night's sleep, Mom. Thanks." She managed a weak smile for her mother before retreating back to her room and shoveling her dinner into her face. She figured she could read for a while and call it a night. Rest seemed like it'd help with both her stomachache and the remnants of her creepy moment from the day before. Wanting a more challenging read than her standard fare, she picked up *The Lottery* by Shirley Jackson. It had been on her summer reading list, but she'd never gotten around to it.

As she read about a small town's violent tradition, Laura drifted off into an uncomfortable sleep, thoughts of brutal humanity jumbled about in her head. That night, her dreams were tortured as she tossed, turned, and whimpered through her unrelenting nightmares. Her brain summoned the buried memories from the time before her parents divorced and brought them right into the fray.

She dreamt of her drunken father screaming and smashing her mother against the wall, slurring his speech and threatening to hurt her more if she didn't stop all her incessant mewling. There were good memories of her father buried somewhere in her brain, but it was always the bad ones that stood strong.

Her father, a hulking figure, threw her much smaller mother down the stairs while Laura hid quietly in her room watching, peeking through the crack of her open door and wishing it would all just stop. She stifled a cry as her mother's crinkled form tumbled and halted at an unnatural angle on the landing at the bottom of the stairwell. Terrified her mother was dead or dying, Laura crept from her room as silently as possible and ran to the hallway telephone to dial 911, but her father spotted her almost immediately. He was bigger and quicker and tore across the house in a blind rage. He used his massive hands to rip the phone from her small, trembling fingers, pulling the entire thing free from the wall, before screaming that she'd better watch her step unless she wanted to wind up like her mother. Laura wasn't old enough for a cell phone and had no other means of communication with the outside world.

Her father leered at her with a triumphant glint on his face as she cautiously retreated to her room, slamming the door and locking it behind her. Had her bladder been full, Laura would have wet herself in fear. Terrified her mother wouldn't wake up, she crept out of her window and tried to signal a neighbor for help. Curtains were drawn and the town was silent, save the electric pop of a streetlight flickering in the night. Eventually, she curled up into a ball crying until her body gave in to the exhaustion she'd built up from the traumatic event. She fell asleep there on the roof landing, directly outside of her window, crusty tears streaking across her round face.

Chapter 4

Laura woke up, thick-tongued and upset, without having recharged during the night. She wept a few tears as memories of her dreams and the real trauma of her past lingered in the morning light. Flickers of her father's angry face blinked across her vision while she made her way back into the waking world. Even after she stopped crying, she felt off, like something was missing, as if someone had poked her with a pin and let some of her humanity deflate overnight. Her old shrink would have called this "numb," but Laura felt a little wicked instead.

Looking to her left, she spotted *The Lottery* and glared at it.

That maybe wasn't the book for me.

Stupid, hateful humanity.

Yuck.

Not wanting to revisit Jackson's story again, she tossed the book into the wastebasket next to her bed. She hated discarding literature, but there was something wrong with that book and she never wanted to see it again. Nothing is worth triggering those nightmares.

The book, she thought, had woken the trauma she'd worked so hard to pack away. All of the awful therapy and talks with her weirdo counselor had helped her push the hurt and anger aside. But here it was, right at the surface again. A raw, oddly vacant feeling settled over

Laura like a scratchy wool blanket, cloaking her every thought and movement.

She resented her father—that much was evident—but dreaming of his misdeeds filled her with an all-consuming rage, and that empty space inside her chest swelled with white-hot anger. When her father started coming home slurring his words, mean and beady-eyed, Laura got angry. She didn't fully understand it, the rage swimming just under her skin. She felt that most little girls would be scared of their violent fathers, but she'd always gotten mad instead. Her anger scared her. She was terrified of ending up mean and violent like him.

That book, she thought, and those dreams had brought her hatred of dear old Dad out of hibernation. "Triggered," her therapist would have called it. Laura felt like she'd regressed into her younger self, that all of the coping tricks she'd learned dissolved a bit overnight too, and that frustrated her beyond belief. She had enough going on in her life and didn't need something else to worry about. She'd promised never to give her father that kind of space in her life again. Breaking that promise pissed her off. She felt disappointed in herself.

"Mom," she called, her voice full of exhaustion and a deep sense of unease.

After a few seconds, her mother tapped lightly on the door. "Everything okay in here?"

Laura hesitated, feeling the memories of her nightmares washing over her again. "No. I had a rough night."

Her mother frowned, seeming troubled. "Nightmares again?"

"Yeah," she confirmed, chest feeling tight. "Dad again. I thought this was over."

Her mother's eyes went wide, softening but also full of worry. "Honey, I'm sorry," she murmured. "This is my fault. I know you've been struggling."

Laura shook her head. "It isn't. It's his fault. Don't blame yourself. You're, like, the best mom ever. He's the monster. This is his fault. I don't want him to get to me like this anymore. I just...don't know how to make the dreams stop." She shuddered, a creeping chill filling her chest as her emotions flared.

"Do you maybe want to see Dr. Yardley again?"

"No, definitely not. She always has white crust in the corners of her mouth, and it was extra gross. Can we just go do something fun today? I think I might need a distraction."

"Sure, kid," she said, straining to smile at her daughter but knowing they shared a deep pain. "Why don't you get dressed, and we can go see a movie and get some burgers."

"Okay, thanks, Mom."

Laura went about her morning routine, dressing and making herself look somewhat human. She even wore her favorite Darth Vader overalls. But she couldn't shake the feeling that something was missing, that her anger was dangerous. Still, she pushed through her negative feelings to spend time with her kind mother.

As they stepped out of the car, Laura could smell buttery popcorn before getting close to the town's small two-screen theater. Despite the turmoil in her head, she loved a good spooky film and a giant tub of movie theater popcorn. "We're seeing the scary one, right?"

"What is it with you and the spooky stuff lately?" her mom asked, playfully elbowing Laura as they entered the theater lobby. "You going goth on me?"

"Don't be weird, Mom. I just like scary things. They make me feel better about life, you know? Monsters aren't scary when they're on the screen. They're controlled and you get to walk away safe and happy in the end."

Her mother didn't know how to take Laura's comment but acquiesced to her request. "The scary one it is. It's PG-13. Think you can manage?"

"Ugh, stop. I'm twelve, almost thirteen. I'll be fine. Don't treat me like a little kid!"

After the movie, they wandered to a cozy diner on the corner of the busy street. A few customers littered the well-worn booths, but most of the diner was open and quiet. Laura and her mother splurged on the special: a giant cheeseburger and halfsies, half onion rings and half fries. While they ate, the conversation flowed easily as Laura recounted her favorite and least favorite parts of the movie they'd seen.

"So, I loved the ghosts. They were super freaky."

"And that's going to help your nightmares how?" her mother asked before popping another French fry in her mouth.

"Mom, ghosts are not real. Why would I be afraid?"

Her mother shrugged and continued listening to Laura's movie review.

"You know what I hated, though?" Laura asked, her face twisted into a mask of disgust.

"What's that?"

"Those idiot girls. They literally did the stupidest thing every single time. No wonder so many of them die in these movies. I'd never just wander out into the dark unarmed and alone. Like, oh hey, come and get me. How dumb! Why can't they put smarter girls in movies like this? It's such an insult."

"And you've just cracked the Hollywood code to success. Stupid people sell movie tickets."

"Well, I would never be that stupid. Ghosts are easy to get rid of," Laura replied, arms crossed and sure of her abilities.

"Okay then. I'll come to you if I ever meet a ghost. Now, finish that soda, and let's get out of here."

Laura nodded, grabbing her glass and slurping the remaining sweet liquid in one gulp. She placed the cup back on the table and let out a noisy burp.

"Gross, Laura."

"You're welcome, Mom," she replied, taking a mock bow at the table.

As her mother was paying the check, Laura caught a glimpse of herself in the window and noticed she looked a little gaunt, haunted even—by her past or her awful father maybe. Or perhaps she was just tired. As they made their way home, Laura tried to stay present in the moment, clinging to the fleeting instances of fun with her mother. But something was still off; she wasn't sure if it was just her nightmares rolling around in the background of her brain or if something else was wrong. Usually, a fun night out with her mom made everything feel better, at least for a while.

Upon returning home, she thanked her mother for a fun day, went upstairs, and got ready for bed before falling into another fitful night of tortured sleep.

Laura woke deep in the night, sweat covering her forehead, darkness engulfing the room. She turned her face, squinting at the neon red glow of the clock on her dresser: 3:00 AM. A quiet shuffling began somewhere in the house, the scrambling sounds getting louder as the seconds ticked by. The sound wasn't human and was too loud for a rodent. They didn't have pets, so noise of any kind was unnatural in the middle of the night unless someone fell asleep watching TV.

Laura opened her mouth to cry out for her mother, but instead of screaming, she only strangled out a quiet puff of air. She didn't want to give her position away or get her mother hurt more than she'd already been. The sound could have been anything, and staying silent felt like her best choice. Petrified, she worried her father had come back to hurt them as the noises stilled and came to a stop outside her bedroom door.

Is it my turn now?

Did he come for me?

Is that why I've been dreaming about him?

Just then, a red light filled the space between her floor and the door, casting a dim, eerie glow across her bedroom carpet. The light didn't fill the entire room, and she knew she was still safely in shadow. But the crimson glow was foreboding and unnatural. She heard something take a step, and two peg-like shadows filtered into and across her room.

As her heart pumped hard against her chest, Laura's fear took over. Her body began to shake uncontrollably, and she broke out into a cold sweat just before she passed out, drifting back into another dark sleep. Seconds before her vision went dark, a thought filled her head as she stared at the peculiar shadow on her floor.

Are those hooves?

Chapter 5

K**NOWING THE NIGHTMARES HADN'T** fully sloughed off upon waking, Laura attempted to hold back the dam long enough to make it through her school day. She needed routine. As much as she hated to admit it, school fulfilled that purpose. She didn't have many friends to distract her from her studies. So, the routine was what she clung to.

"We've got to leave in 15, kid. Get down here."

"Crap," she said, before running to her closet and tossing on her favorite *Goosebumps* t-shirt, the one with Slappy the ventriloquist dummy on the front. She grabbed a pair of worn-in, dirty jeans from the floor and gave them the sniff test before deciding they seemed okay to wear. Glancing at her clock, she panicked and grabbed her book bag before flying down the stairs.

Her mother stood near the door, a warm Pop-Tart in her hand. "You really cut these things close. It's a good thing I always make an extra one of these." She handed Laura the pastry before ushering her out the door and into the car.

They drove to school in a companionable silence. "Try to have a good day, kiddo," her mother offered as she was hopping out, dreading a long day back in school. She didn't say it, but Laura could tell by the plastic look on her face that her mom was still worried.

Putting on her best pretend smile, Laura beamed at her mother, hoping to put some of her worries to rest. "I'll do my best."

"Laura, are you paying attention?" Mrs. Sharp, her least favorite teacher, snipped.

"Um...yes," she replied, snapping her eyes to the front of the room. She'd been lost in thought while her shrill teacher pranced across the front of the room talking down to everyone in her whiny sneer of a voice. They were learning fractions, but Laura had missed much of last week's lessons because Mrs. Sharp would dump the contents of her desk on the floor if even one scrap of paper stuck out or if the desk was even a centimeter ajar. As someone who struggled with basic organization, Laura suffered this consequence almost every day. She tried to stay tidy, but could never make everything fit into the ancient wooden desk. As a result, she'd fallen behind, and much of what the teacher was saying made no sense to her. Mrs. Sharp's haughty demeanor made it clear that she thought herself better than everyone in the room, and Laura wondered why people like this decided teaching was their calling.

"Then can you answer the question? We don't have all day." The teacher beelined toward Laura and clacked her long nails on her newly organized desk.

"No."

"What do you mean, no? Do you not know the answer? We've been going over this for days. Do you hear that, folks? It sounds like our friend Laura hasn't been paying attention in class."

Looking up at Mrs. Sharp, hot anger coursing through her veins, Laura snapped back, "Can you just pick on someone else today? I'm not in the mood for this. I have enough problems without you trying to make me feel dumb." After speaking, she clapped her hands over her mouth in disbelief. While she hated Mrs. Sharp, she was usually calm and respectful anyway.

Mrs. Sharp's rodent-like mouth hung open. "Excuse me, young lady? Do you want to go to the principal's office instead?"

The classroom chatter halted as eyes turned to the battle of wills happening at Laura's desk. "Sure," she replied. "It can't be worse than this. Maybe Principal Clifton wants to know about how you angrily dump our desks upside down when you're stumbling around the room. Maybe he wants to sniff your coffee too." Laura's eyes went wide. She felt as if something else was controlling the words coming out of her mouth. She didn't want to keep digging a hole, but she couldn't help it.

"You will not speak to me that way," Mrs. Sharp demanded, her face reddening, likely a mixture of anger and embarrassment.

Laura shook her head, trying to shake off the attitude, but instead, she sneered at her awful teacher. "I will. I'm done with your abuse. We all are. No one in this room deserves to be made to feel stupid. Do you feel good about yourself? Is terrorizing children giving your self-esteem a boost? You may need to consider another profession."

Mrs. Sharp's hands balled into angry little fists, but she said nothing as she stomped away, seeming defeated. "Someone answer my question so we can get on with the lesson," she demanded.

As Seraphine, a red-headed math whiz, tentatively raised her hand to answer the question, Laura realized she felt better after letting some of her anger out into the world.

Maybe I should fight back more often.

Maybe it'll help with the nightmares.

But as the day wore on, Laura began to feel off again. Something weird wriggled along under her skin. It was almost like she was fracturing in two, like two different Lauras lived in her head: the normal, quiet one who let monsters like her math teacher walk all over her, and the sly one who used her guile to watch awful people squirm.

Regardless of the strange war happening in her body, Laura was able to keep from another outburst and felt a little embarrassed she'd let Mrs. Sharp get to her in such a way, but she found even her favorite teachers grating. She also wanted to punch the oafish boy who sat next to her in science class picking his nose, seemingly mining for gold. Laura had never punched anyone before, and the thought made her briefly wonder if she was going to be monstrous in the way her father was. It shook her to the core.

I need to get a hold of myself. I will not be like that man.

Not now.

Not ever.

I don't care if it's in my genes.

I won't do it.

The store was closed for inventory, and her mother always finished the task by mid-afternoon. So Laura was able to hop on a school bus and head straight home. Upon arriving at her house, she went straight up to her room, wanting to avoid her mother as long as possible. She didn't want her mom to see her this way, to compare her to her awful father. Her room, she thought, was a safe haven for now, and she wondered if a sweet treat would right all the gloom that had settled on her shoulders over the course of the day.

That's what people do, right?

They eat to feel better.

Her mother's rounder face was evidence of that.

"It's nice to see you too," her mother yelled as Laura raced up the stairs to her room.

She whipped her backpack on the floor, noticing the clean and shiny tin sitting on her bed, and called down to thank her mother for washing it.

"You're welcome, honey. I'm glad you like your new toy."

Feeling somewhat ravenous, Laura readied her mix and spread it out in the pan, plugged in her oven, and shoved the batter in. Once it came out, she noticed red ooze bubbling like lava and flowing from the cracks that had erupted on the cake's surface—*still weird*—but she greedily slurped down the strange mixture anyway. Even though she'd had a tummy ache last night, her need for something dark and sugary won out. Ashy, though sweet, the treat satisfied her and made her brain go fuzzy. She felt a momentary sense of peace before her stomach twisted, causing her legs to buckle. Her stomach burned, an odd tenderness that almost felt like a bruise, and the displeasing sensation began to spread across her torso and out to her extremities.

Darkness clawed at the edges of her vision as she slumped down toward the floor, cold sweat on her brow. While she lay writhing there on the floor, clammy and afraid, Laura was certain she could hear a deep chuckle off in the distance.

"Are you okay up there?" her mother called from downstairs, having heard a decisive thump from above.

Through gritted teeth, she replied, "I'm fine, Mom... Dropped something..."

"Okay, well, be careful, ya klutz, and don't spoil your dinner too much. I can smell you baking again. Thought you didn't like that thing?"

Laura didn't reply as the pain ramped up, turning fiery and all-consuming. She could feel her rational thoughts quieting in the background, leaving room for her new bold self to take over and drive for a while. As she curled further into a tight ball, the booming chuckle filled her ears again.

"Poor little lamb," said the disembodied voice. "You're not looking well."

Laura covered her ears, trying to stifle the speaking. It was deep and eerie. She felt like someone was talking directly to her brain. It made her feel unwell in an entirely different way, like she'd rolled around in mud and fell asleep caked in grime. The voice made her want to retch.

"You should set your anger free. See how powerful you really are."

Get out of my head.

I'm not crazy.

You're not real.

Go away. Leave me alone.

With a final chuckle, the voice faded, and along with it, Laura's pain faded too. She brought herself up to her knees and caught a glimpse of herself in the mirror. Her reflection was changing, slightly warped. She was confident that her teeth were sharper than before, just a little, and she spotted and then felt strange bumps above each of her ears.

Great, I probably have a concussion. Mom's going to be mad if she sees these. Ughhhhhh...

What a terrible day.

She used her sleeve to wipe away the tepid sweat from her face. Eventually, she pulled herself all the way back up and slogged to the bathroom to splash cool water on her face. Examining herself in the bright vanity lights, she poked at the tender bumps on her head and groaned. When she felt more together and calmed down a little, she pulled on a knit cap and wore it throughout dinner to help disguise her injury. She couldn't stomach the idea of her mother fretting over her or making her go to a noisy Urgent Care clinic to be prodded by an overworked doctor. Keeping her mom as stress free as possible was Laura's life goal, but selfishly she also wanted to be left alone in her misery with her head trauma.

While the hat was an odd fashion choice, her mother barely noticed. They ate together, sharing highlights from the day, and retired to their own rooms in a companionable silence. Laura's feigning well had paid off, and her mother was able to relax and slough off the stress of inventory by having a glass of wine and continuing her *SVU* binge while Laura trudged back up to bed, hoping for dreamless sleep, and to wake up feeling like her normal self again.

Chapter 6

Unfortunately, as Laura slept that night, her dark dreams returned. Once the black static behind her eyelids cleared, she found herself watching another episode of her father's late-night screaming. This, she thought, was the worst TV show in existence. She didn't want it in syndication. She didn't want to see these reruns. Laura knew she'd endured these scenes in her waking life and wanted nothing to do with a nighttime replay, but she had no say in what channel her brain was playing tonight.

This time, her father punched a hole into the wall near a photo from a family trip they'd taken to Six Flags, back when her parents were all smiles in front of her and kept their arguing to a quiet lull behind closed doors. Laura remembered the day. It was her first time riding the Shock Wave. She'd tried the year before, but wasn't quite tall enough. When they got to the front of the line, her father stomped and scoffed, leaving her behind to wait while he rode the coaster. But she hadn't inconvenienced him this time, and they rode together, laughing and screaming down larger drops and loop-de-loops. The good memories were few and far between, but that day at Six Flags had been wholesome and fun.

But in the dream, she was at home where her father slammed the front door, storming out in a rage and disappearing until the following day. She had no idea where he'd gone—maybe to another bar, maybe somewhere worse. She only knew that after tucking her in, red-faced and bleary-eyed, her mother cried herself to sleep. She could hear the soft mewling through the flimsy drywall or wafting up the vents. This memory was less violent than some of her others. Her dad hadn't physically harmed her mom during the bout, but judging by all the tears, her mother was still hurting pretty badly. Laura learned that night that abuse wasn't always physical, that words and actions could hurt as much as punches and slaps. While less remarkable than some memories of her father, this one had burned itself into Laura's brain, another puzzle piece of violence and shame.

She awoke slick with sweat, in screaming pain, sometime close to midnight. Her body felt foreign and wrong as she attempted to make sense of her surroundings. Her mother had given her "The Talk" and she worried this was part of her changing body; she also pleaded to whatever deity was listening that it wasn't. She wasn't ready for that, and she didn't think she could handle this kind of pain every month for the rest of her days.

No, thank you.

Pass.

The room seemed to spin around her. Odd shadows danced across the ceiling, and a sliver of moonlight lit the room just enough to creep her out. The tree branches waved like outstretched fingers, all aimed at Laura, all seeming to judge her. Being jolted from sleep, her pulse racing, she was on the defensive. She never felt safe in darkness, but this was a new level of awful.

Searing pain shot through her skull, causing her hands to fly up to the sides of her head in an attempt to stifle the sensation. Her tiny fingers grazed something hard, slightly jagged, and definitely unnatural. The strange bumps she'd disguised at dinner had ripped through the flesh of her scalp, forming into bony protrusions, one on each side of her head. Panic coursed through her veins as she attempted to understand the impossible situation in which she found herself. Shooting up from her bed, she scrambled her way across the room to her mirrored dresser to inspect the lumps she was certain she felt atop her head.

Laura looked in the mirror, metallic-tasting blood in her mouth, sure that her teeth had not been as razor-sharp yesterday. She checked her mouth for sores, but saw only red gums and pointy, jagged incisors.

That's definitely new. Those are full-blown fangs.

What the hell?

Am I a vampire now?

Her breath stilled, and she stifled a scream when she finally spied the gnarled horns sprouting from her skull, twisted and outstretched like a zombie's hand digging its way out of a useless grave.

What the hell?

Her hands, too, were covered in blood smears and clumps of hair.

This has to be a dream. This is just another nightmare.

Wake up, Laura.

Wake up.

She pinched herself.

Ouch, what the heck? It's not supposed to hurt while you're asleep.

Laura forced her eyes away from the monster in the mirror. It looked like her, but her brain couldn't reconcile the image as actually being her. Still, no matter how hard she tried to convince herself that this was another twisted dream or, perhaps, a stress delusion, she couldn't shake the feeling that something was happening to her, like she'd befallen an evil curse.

"At least it's not my period," she joked, attempting to quell her fear. None of what she saw was logical or even sane, and she worried she was having a break from reality.

I'm going back to sleep now.

This isn't happening. It can't be real.

It's just some kind of awful brain trickery.

She trudged back to bed, the pounding in her head thumping a bit more with each step. Lying still, the pain eased enough for Laura to get a few more hours of sleep. The rest of the night passed in a blur of horrid nightmares of her father and his various violent misdeeds, each one worse than the one before. His bloated face, twisted into a mask of rage, emblazoned itself on the backs of her eyelids. She'd never forget the malice in his eyes, the sheer danger and cruelty. In her dreams, she tried to scream, to run from his anger, but he stood there at every turn, menacing and horrid. She feared his bad nature was infiltrating her, corrupting her, making her more like him. But even in her dream-like state, she was dead set on not being him. She wanted to destroy him instead. The dream world made her feel lost in some sort of mental maze of her own creation, and she ached for the sweet release of morning's sunlight.

By daybreak, Laura was rattled, still exhausted after her night of restless dreaming. She shook there under her covers; not from cold, but from fear of facing her demons, of facing herself. She was terrified that the dark inside her was, in fact, more than a trick of the mind, that it was oozing out of her and turning her into a literal monster. As she lay in bed, sun grazing her skin, she felt grateful that she was not, in fact, a vampire.

Part of her hoped the middle of the night freak-out had been a dream, but the way her teeth felt against her tongue confirmed that at least part of the night had been real. She still had odd, sharpened incisors.

Her fears were confirmed when she caught a glimpse of herself in the mirror.

"Oh, oh no."

Chapter 7

As Laura stared at her foreign face in the mirror, examining the demonic horns, she noted that the pain had at least passed sometime during the night. The horns and teeth, though, remained. Glancing back at her bed, she noticed a few small smears of blood, but no real evidence of the transformation. Even her hands had been wiped clean at some point during the night.

She ran her hands curiously over the sandpapery ridges of the horns. Everything felt pointy, and her visibly extended canines caused her to speak with a slight lisp. "Thisss isssn't okay. None of thisss isss okay."

She stomped her foot in a rage before breaking down in deep, wracking sobs. Though firmly in pre-teen territory, she needed her mom more than she had in years. She thought her mom had prepared her for the horror of womanhood. She knew to expect body changes at her age, but she'd never been warned something like this could happen. Boobs, yes. Periods, sure. Demonic horns and fangs, no way. It was impossible. You don't just see people walking around with fully formed horns, not in her small town anyway. Feeling like a small child again, she ran down to her mother for help and was met with bewilderment.

"Mom, I need help!" she screamed, racing into the kitchen where her mother was drowsily sipping a steaming cup of coffee.

"What? What's going on? Slow down. Where's the fire?"

"Just look at me!" she said, pointing to her head and opening her mouth wide.

"Are you sick? Do you have a fever? I hope this isn't strep again. You just had it. We do not need a repeat." Her mother reached out, placing the back of her hand on Laura's forehead. "No, you don't feel warm. What's going on? I'm not awake enough for whatever this is."

"Mom," Laura gasped, incredulous. "I have horns. Right here." She exaggeratedly pointed at the sides of her head.

"What are you talking about, Laura? Of course you don't have horns. Is this some kind of TikTok prank? You've gotta let me fully wake up before hitting me with this stuff." Her mother collapsed back into her chair, fading once again into her groggy morning stance. She sipped her scalding coffee before looking back up at her child.

Trying not to break out into further panic, Laura took a few deep breaths before opening her mouth and addressing her mother again. "You really don't see them? Look at my teeth. Do they look normal to you?"

Her mother leaned in to examine Laura's mouth. "They look like they need a good brushing, but other than that, yep, super normal." She waved her arm in a pee-ew gesture.

Not stopping to engage with her mother's infantile gesture, Laura replied, "Are you sure?"

"Definitely," her mother said, eyeing her suspiciously. "Is everything okay? You can be honest with me. I'm really starting to worry about you, kid. You've been all kinds of funky these last few days. I don't know what this whole production is about," she said, vaguely gesturing toward her child, "but it's definitely not normal."

Laura looked at her mom, unsure of what to say or do, as tears welled up in her eyes. She needed help, but she wasn't sure where to get it, especially when her story was so inconceivable. Instead of responding to her mother, she turned and bolted back upstairs as the tears flowed freely from her face.

"Laura, where are you going? We're not done talking."

Laura raced back to her bedroom mirror, needing to confirm whether or not she was crazy, but when she got there, her monstrous teeth and horns were staring right back at her. Gone was the youthful freckled face she was used to seeing every morning.

Am I ill? Is this what a breakdown feels like?

Can anyone help me now?

Instead of facing her mother, she called back downstairs, doing her best to use an even and metered tone, "Can I stay home today, Mom?"

No response, but a few minutes later, her mother appeared at the doorway, worry evident on her face. "Are you still feeling sick in your stomach?"

"No, but I think I have sharp teeth and horns. So maybe I'm not entirely well."

Laura's mother wasn't certain what was going on with her daughter, but she was still concerned. Laura could tell, even though her mother was trying to dismiss the behavior as silly childhood antics. Rolling her eyes, the girl's mother frowned and disregarded the behavior. Instead of seeing it as an actual problem, she questioned her child. "Do you have a paper due? Is that what this is about? Are you being bullied? Has someone offered you drugs? Do we need to circle back about the dead animals?"

"No, Mom, I have frickin' horns! Don't you see these giant beasties spiraling behind my ears?"

She laughed, seeming less and less concerned for her daughter with each passing moment. She presumed Laura was still playing at something, and she relented. "Do you also have a tail? Ah, yes, there it is, swishing about behind you. Can you fling stuff with it? You know, I've always wanted a tail myself!"

"Mom, that's not funny! I'm having a crisis. I need a mental health day."

Her mother shrugged. "Sure, you haven't had a day off in a while. Why didn't you just say that in the first place? You know I would give you the day off. Middle school can wait, just for today. Will you be okay while I'm at work? Do you want me to close the shop or call Aunt Peggy to cover for me? We can have a girl's day again. That might be nice."

"No, Mom. You can go to work. I'll be fine here, I hope."

Her mother raised an eyebrow at her. "You hope? You're not exactly inspiring confidence, though."

"Seriously, Mom. I'll be okay. I think it's these nightmares rattling me."

Her mother softened again. "Let's just check you out to make sure you're not actually sick before I leave. Okay?" Ever the vigilant mother, she took Laura's temperature, just for good measure, and made sure she ate something healthy for breakfast before heading to work and leaving Laura to her own devices.

"Okay, kid. Please call if you need something. I'll bring home Chinese tonight. How's that sound?"

"Good. Thanks, Mom. Cashew chicken for me. I'm just going to relax again today. Maybe I'm just stressed out."

"You're definitely stressed out. No maybes there. You should re-think seeing the doctor again. We can discuss it later. But for now, relax and enjoy the day. You're going to school tomorrow, with or without horns."

Laura nodded, not wanting to freak out on her mom. She stood in the living room waving goodbye as her mother exited the house. Once alone, Laura began to pace the upstairs hallway, back and forth, back and forth. The carpet wore down, showing the track of her pacing. Despite her best efforts, she could feel steamy anger welling up inside of her once more.

"What's happening to me?"

I think you know, came a disembodied voice, existing somewhere in Laura's head. It had been the same voice for days, that rough and booming cadence, filled to the brim with condescension.

"I don't though. I don't know anything. What do you want? Who are you? Are you even real?"

You do. You will. This is what you were meant for. I am very real. Don't worry, we'll be meeting soon.

Laura pushed the voice away, thinking her brain was playing more tricks on her. "Get out and stay out," she said, snapping the mental door shut.

You can ignore me for now, but I'll be back.

The voice stilled while Laura grasped for an answer. The only thing she knew for sure was that things were changing and things were not right.

"Horns. I have literal monster horns, but no one else can see them. What the hell?"

She wished the woman who'd foisted the oven off on her was still camped across the street from her mother's shop, but she'd disappeared the day after their exchange. She had a feeling the woman knew more than she'd said.

Chapter 8

"Maybe I do need to go back to the doctor? Maybe Mom can get me another doctor? That last one clearly didn't do the trick if I'm hallucinating." Pacing the floor again, Laura tried to harmonize what she saw in the mirror with what her mom clearly had not seen, and she couldn't come up with any logical explanation for her monstrous appearance. She could see and feel the horns. They'd given her pain. Reaching up to feel them one more time, she was unsurprised when she grasped the firm rough surface of her new horns. "I can feel them. How could they be an illusion?"

Not knowing what to do, she went back to her room and found the contents of her Easy-Bake disaster still strewn about the floor, though she had remembered to unplug the odd toy.

"At least I didn't burn the house down. I'd definitely be in trouble then." She laughed nervously, trying to pretend things were back to normal.

The girl took a moment to look around her room, glancing at all of her bits and baubles. It was the room of an average, albeit slightly odd, 12-year-old girl. She had clearly been influenced by her mother's dedication to power ballads and 80s rock and roll. Despite everything she had been through, and all of the negativity, she had come out on top. She was alive. She could smile. Her mother, too, made it out of the darkness mostly intact. The fact that things were going off the rails now just didn't make sense to Laura.

Wanting to keep her hands busy and her brain distracted, Laura decided to make her third and final devil's food cake.

"Everything's better with a little snack, right?"

She went about mechanically preparing the batter and mixing the cake, shoved it into the oven with her plastic wand, and pushed it back out again when it was cooked through. The scent of chocolate and slightly burnt sugar filled her bedroom. The simple task soothed her nerves as she mindlessly went through the motions.

This time, though, the cake looked different. There was no red; instead, it looked dry and ashen, with deep cracks running across the surface of her confection.

"Weird. Did I actually burn it? I don't think so. They all smelled like this. Maybe it's past its expiration date?" She sniffed it again for good measure, but decided it seemed fine.

She shrugged and popped the cake out—in one piece this time—before savoring the rich, chocolatey flavor. It didn't taste burnt. In fact, this was the best one yet. Even better, no pain came as she ate. She wondered if she'd just had some type of tummy bug and that cramping after her previous cakes was a coincidence, but after a few moments, her head grew foggy. It was almost like the time she had to have a broken tooth pulled. They didn't put her to sleep, but they gave her something to make her feel...loopy. Briefly, she wondered if she was having an allergic reaction to the cakes themselves. Perhaps that would account for the way her stomach had been feeling, as well as the odd hallucinations.

Maybe these things are doing something weird to me.
Maybe I shouldn't have taken cakes from a stranger.
Maybe the cakes are full of drugs.

Still, she kept eating, piling each chunk into her mouth, masticating it, and swallowing until every crumb had worked its way into her aching belly. She didn't even want to eat it. Try as she might, though, she still ate every last bite of that ashy-looking chocolate cake. Now certain there was something wrong with the cakes and worried she'd been poisoning herself for the last few days, she felt stupid for having taken the toy from the crazy old woman in the first place.

"Who does that? It's literally the first rule in the book. Don't take candy from strangers."

Anyone with a lick of sense would have tossed out at least the cake mixes. Laura liked to think she was grown up, but she couldn't even stop eating a stupid poison cake. Something had compelled her to keep going. Her hand and mouth were working independently of her brain. She had been screaming at herself to stop, but nothing happened. She just ate and ate and ate until the cake was gone, flushed down to the pit of her belly, sitting in her stomach acids and waiting for digestion.

An odd sensation began in her feet, tingling and warm. The fuzzy feeling traveled up her legs, and after a few moments, Laura gasped for breath. Something hard and rotten had landed deep in her chest. Briefly, she wondered if this was what a heart attack felt like. Maybe that's what the poison eventually did. After a few seconds, though, the vise-like grip on her heart released. But something in her had changed. She felt gray, as if her goodness was being sucked from her bones, and strangely she enjoyed this new sensation. Over the past few days, she had thought there were two Lauras. One was the good, kindly Laura that everyone had grown to know and at least tolerate. The other felt soulless and hungry for revenge. As she pondered her circumstances, Laura failed to notice what was happening to her body.

She floated off, now outside of her body, watching a peculiar scene unfold before her. She saw herself standing, almost propelled by an unseen force. Her body took clumsy steps, moving to her closet and dressing for an outing before heading out of the room and into the hall. Her clothes weren't as coordinated as she'd have liked, but they were at least weather-appropriate. She dressed in long sleeves, comfortable sweatpants, and made sure to zip up her favorite vest. She would at least be protected from the cooler fall temperatures. As she floated there, an observer, she wondered if her body was on autopilot or if she was perhaps being puppeteered by someone or something else. At this point, anything was possible. Would she be trapped like this, a discombobulated soul, damned to watch her mortal form move about and grow old without her inside of it? Had she died? Is this what ghost life was like? Laura had no idea what was going on, but instead of freaking out, she felt mellow and decided to float along with the flow to see what would happen next. Her anger was suddenly and interestingly missing as she followed along with her corporeal form. Floating, though she couldn't feel the sensation, must have been a stress reliever.

Unbeknownst to her, something old and dark was compelling her to move. In eating those three devil's food cakes, she'd entered into a covenant with the dark lord himself.

"Not only is this extremely weird, it feels very sinister."

Now you're getting it, kid.

"What the heck was that? Get out of my head. I must be going crazy!"

Her attention drifted back to the strange agreement she made with the bedraggled woman across the street from her mother's shop, and the oddly precise wording the old woman had made her agree to. Was that a pact of sorts?

Bingo!

This time, she ignored the deep voice in her head. She had agreed to take the toy of her own accord. She did agree to eat one cake per day. There must have been fine print somewhere, but Laura certainly hadn't read it.

That'll get ya every time.

"Seriously, get out of my head! I don't need any intrusive thoughts right now. I've got enough going on."

She winced, her body flinching, as it grabbed a sharp blade from the knife block on top of the kitchen counter. For a second, she was back inside herself and staring at her knife-filled hand. A second later, she returned to floating along above herself.

Whoa. What just happened? Did I do that?

Why do I have a knife?

What is going on?

After the momentary glitch, Laura's body steadied again and hid the gleaming blade within the folds of her puffy purple vest.

She didn't know what was happening to her, but these actions weren't her idea; at least, not all her idea. However, she continued to hover in her bodiless form, enchanted by the ordeal. Not that she had a choice in the matter. She flew along, hovering in the sky and admiring the ability to see the world from a new perspective. In those last few minutes, her fear had disappeared, and she was more curious now than afraid.

I wonder where we're going.

As her body moved to the door and out onto the sidewalk in front of the house, Laura was pulled along as if she were a kite floating on the wind with an unseen string tethering her to the empty form wandering down the block.

"Good morning, Laura," a voice called from across the street. It was Mrs. Roth, one of her busybody neighbors. Laura raised her ghostly fingers, momentarily distracted by the fact that they were see-through. She waved at Mrs. Roth but, of course, was not seen. Her shell of a body simply lumbered forward, paying no attention to the frumpy woman calling her name.

"Laura?" came the now concerned voice of Mrs. Roth. "Laura, is everything alright?" she yelled, attempting to grab Laura's attention. The look on her face was a mix of confusion and concern with just a hint of annoyance.

Laura's body gave no response. It just took clunky steps farther down the road and away from Mrs. Roth's straining voice.

Mrs. Roth rushed inside her home in a hurry, leaving Laura alone with herself. Laura wondered why the woman didn't give chase, but there was nothing she could do to affect the situation. She called out a quick "sorry" from her ghostly mouth even though she clearly wasn't visible to anyone else, or at least not to Mrs. Roth.

Laura's odd, wispy form continued being dragged farther down the road. She felt like one of those Thanksgiving Day parade blimps, bobbing along down the street, tethered to Earth by invisible strings. Curiously, the longer her body shambled along and the farther she went from her home, the closer she was pulled to the ground, as if something was reeling in the invisible kite strings that kept her suspended in the sky. While her body moved farther away from her home, her floating form came back down to earth, eventually walking behind her physical body in an odd pantomime.

What in the world?

Chapter 9

As Laura's body stomped down the street and into town, she was pulled forward into the soulless shell of her physical body. Momentarily, she felt screaming pain followed by dizziness and more pressure than she was comfortable with, as if her own body was trying to eject her. But after a few moments, she was looking through her eye sockets again, her ghost form joined with her automaton body.

Now that was a wild ride.

She picked up one of her hands and examined it, flexing her fingers in and out to ensure she was back in control of herself. She jumped a few times, and her body seemed to respond as well as it ever had. Things seemed to be moving normally enough.

She turned her hand over and examined the skin. While it was definitely her hand, marked with a crescent scar between her right thumb and pointer finger, it also felt somewhat foreign. There was something off, different, and aside from the horns and teeth, she wasn't sure what had just happened. Part of her still felt this was the break from reality she'd suspected before, that she'd finally lost control and let her mental health decline to the point of no return. But the rest of her felt like she was still sane enough and that something unnatural was happening in the world around her.

She realized her emotions, too, had changed, evolved maybe. Instead of feeling cut off from herself, she now felt joined. The two

Lauras were finally united and she was whole again. Her acceptance of something strong and sinister, something to fight off the bad guys, seemed to be what had reunited her with her body. Together, the old and new Laura happily wandered the remaining three blocks to her town's center. She'd gone farther than she realized and was impressed with the amount of ground she'd covered in such a short time. She thought that floating was a much better way to travel than walking. If she had walked all this way from home, her feet would be aching, and she'd be a little sweaty. But her body had lumbered along without the weight of her soul dragging it down, which left her feet feeling springy and new and gave her a renewed sense of energy to continue on in her journey.

While she hadn't been in her body when it started the trek to town, Laura felt certain she knew where they were headed. This was the way to the salvage yard. She'd walked the path a hundred times before. For her, the yard once held adventure and mystery, but that had been muddied these last few years. Since her body seemed to have a plan, she was content to continue on toward the salvage yard, even though she was slightly afraid because she knew who was there waiting. She shuddered, thinking back to her recent nightmares of her father and all his violent misdeeds. Seeing the man face to face would be another level of hell, but it's where her body wanted to go, and she knew she had a knife firmly tucked in her clothing as protection. Pausing again to consider her new realizations, she no longer felt afraid. "Huh, how odd."

She thought she would still tremble when thinking about the awful man. She knew she should. But that reaction was suspiciously absent. While she was willing to go along with what her body had been planning, Laura opted to take the long path. She needed more time to try and puzzle out what she was doing, and to ready and steady herself for whatever that happened to be. In addition to that, the shorter route would have taken her directly past her mother's store, and she didn't want to risk getting spotted, not after she'd weaseled her way out of school.

Her mom would not be happy, and she'd probably get grounded. She hated it when her mom tried to punish her. It was always weird and way too severe for the offense. Laura wasn't in trouble often, so her mother had never really developed the ability to properly punish her. If she was caught red-handed stealing cookies from the cookie jar, it was two weeks of lockdown. The first time she failed a math test, Laura tried to doctor the grade with a red marker of her own. The attempt was pathetic, and her mother saw through it immediately. The punishment for this was two months of grounding, and a conference with her math teacher, Mrs. Sharp. Of course, this was before Laura had opened up to her mother about the cruel things she was enduring at the hand of Mrs. Sharp. Once Laura's mother learned about what was going on in that classroom, she was more sympathetic to Laura and her decisions. However, Laura stopped her mother from interfering for fear of retaliation from the teacher. So that particular pickle had yet to be solved.

After her bout of daydreaming, Laura came back to the here and now. She was hoping her neighbor, Mrs. Roth, hadn't called her mother and gotten her all riled up. Her mom didn't need to deal with whatever this was, and Laura would feel guilty if she caught her close to the salvage yard with a sharpened weapon at her side. That wouldn't look good for anyone, and Laura didn't want to be caught betraying her mother's trust. For these reasons, she stayed on the long path, straying as far from her mother's shop as possible.

Plus, the long way would take Laura through the town's defunct train tunnel and across an overgrown abandoned golf course. She was less likely to be spotted going that way. The fewer paths she crossed, the better. She didn't want to be questioned by any suspicious adults, wondering why she wasn't in school, and she knew someone would stop her if she was spotted. Small towns were annoying sometimes. Laura felt like she could easily sidestep one or two passersby, but she didn't want to risk being caught or being seen by someone she knew. The long path was the better bet if she was set on making it to the salvage yard.

As she picked her way across town, she only ran across one older teen who was sparking up and smoking something skunky near the train tunnel. This side of town was quiet, almost still, and she enjoyed plucking her way through overgrown weeds as she moved closer and closer to her destination.

Laura spied the yard's towering chain link fence in the distance, and if she squinted, she could make out the bright yellow *No Trespassing* sign. She knew she'd find Skimbleshanks, a ragged German shepherd, at the gate. While many feared him, Laura did not. She'd known him since he was a puppy, and he'd never dare to hurt her. He was all bark and very little bite, especially when you gave him a snack and a belly rub.

Once at the gate, Laura flipped the code box cover down and punched in *1203*, her birthday. Her father wasn't the sentimental sort, and he hadn't set up the gate code. Instead, when the lock was installed, her mother made up and set the code. Her drunken father, however, was too lazy to have changed it.

The gate clicked open with a squeal and a rusty pop, allowing her entry into the private business. Skimbleshanks waited, dozing nearby under a lean-to, shielded from the sun. Instead of wagging and racing to greet her, he whimpered and scrambled backward farther into the lean-to, cowering in her presence.

"Hey, boy, I'm not going to hurt you. It's just me. Don't be afraid." The dog stayed away, watching her with wary eyes. "I'm sorry it's been so long. I'll come more often," she offered before moving closer to the makeshift front office, an aging trailer, and away from the dog who she guessed could see her horns. People always say that dogs are perceptive in that way.

Somewhere inside her head, Laura's more authentic, more human voice cried out, *Why did we come here with a knife? What am I doing?*

"Shhh... We're different now," she said to herself in a whispered hush.

Once she reached the trailer and climbed the three steps to the front door, Laura turned the knob, opened the door, and stepped into her father's place of work.

Chapter 10

THE DOOR CREAKED OPEN, but if her father noticed, he made no move to acknowledge the sound. She saw the back of his head, his matted brown hair, and shuddered, memories of her nightmares washing over her. She hadn't seen him in months, and that was her preference. He'd made no effort to see her, and she liked it that way, hoped it would continue indefinitely. They were doing just fine, she and her mother. Laura was not interested in spending her time with such a despicable man. She could never forgive what he'd put her mother through, what she'd been through.

She took a step into the stagnant trailer and slammed the door behind her. Startled, her father nearly fell out of his rickety chair.

"Shit," he yelled before swiveling the chair her way. His eyes narrowed as he spotted Laura. After hiccupping, he addressed her in his drunken and condescending tone, "Daughter. What are you doing here? I don't have time for you." He waved her off and turned back to whatever he had been doing before.

"I'm not here for that. I'm not interested in taking up any of your precious time," Laura replied, balling her hands into fists at her sides.

The man turned around with a sneer on his face. His haughty expression only made Laura more upset. He didn't even seem human. Then again, she didn't seem human herself. Perhaps her new acquisitions were the result of his shoddy genetics. He cleared his throat but did not speak, looking to Laura to make the first move.

Laura squealed, fear filling her pre-teen brain. But her body stood firm and unafraid as it reached into her pocket to remove the knife she'd taken from the kitchen. Her brain and body were working independently in an awkward, cramped shuffle, but Laura held firmly to the knife and was committed to letting the new strong part of her drive.

"And what do you plan to do with that?" her father asked, his voice lilting in amusement. He rose from his chair, wobbling a bit, and closed in on Laura.

Slow to respond, her terrified brain couldn't process what was happening. She'd never been a direct victim of her father's drunken rage. Her mother had always been there as a buffer, a protector. But now she stood face to face with the man who'd caused all of her trauma. Her father reached back with his large open palm, a wind-up, and he slapped Laura hard in the face. The blow caused her to lose grip of the knife, letting it clatter to the floor.

"That'll teach you," her father began, slurring his words. "You never were worth much, were you? I'd have at least respected you if you tried to come at me with that knife. You're just a failure, a worthless use of space, like your hag of a mother."

The white-hot rage that'd filled her vision the last few days boiled over, and just as she was going to read her father the riot act, time stopped.

The tick-tock of the clock ceased its steady background rhythm, and her father stood frozen in an odd position, his face so much less human than she'd remembered. She thought he'd been fun and kind when she was a smaller child, but she wasn't sure her memories were trustworthy. The man who stood before her—lip curled into an ugly, rage-filled half-smile, unkempt patches of facial hair, and almost inhuman, hate-filled eyes—certainly didn't seem fun or kind. She walked up to him, cocking her head to the side to examine him up close. Uncertain how she had come from such a despicable character, Laura stepped back again, having had her fill of his ugly, twisted face.

Looking around, Laura was enchanted by the stillness surrounding her. Little flecks of dust hung in the air, a snapshot of this moment. The dimly lit trailer was like a memory brought to life, a moment in time frozen in place. But instead of looking at a photo, she was experiencing it in real-time.

"Wild," she said, astonished instead of afraid of the scene in front of her. The peculiarity of the trailer, with light cascading in through the slits in the blinds, served as a brief distraction from the awful man in front of her. She felt the warmth of a magic moment embracing her in the seemingly most unlikely of places.

She looked up at her father, frozen in anger, and stepped forward to poke him in his awful face. "You're not so scary now," she said before kicking him hard in the shin. "Whatcha gonna do, old man?"

While he didn't move, she was filled with glee at having inflicted some pain on him in return. She hoped he could feel it, every throbbing second of pain. As she was winding up to slap him in the face like he had done to her moments ago, she was interrupted by a familiar voice behind her.

"Ehhh...emm..." came the clearing of the deep voice she'd been hearing for days. "Having fun, I see."

As Laura turned, she came face to face with a large, ominous figure, a giant beast of a man. Sort of. While humanoid in appearance, the tall, broad figure had great spiraling horns protruding from both sides of his angled head. His skin was bright red and glistened in the dim light of the trailer.

That's the Devil.

Laura gulped before slowly backing away from the terrible crea-ture, uncertain where she could go while she was pinned between her father's frozen body and the demon in front of her. "Uhhhhhhh..."

"You've nothing to fear from me, child. Do not let my appearance fool you. We both know who the true monster is here," he said, point-ing a long-taloned finger at her father.

"I...uh..." Laura stammered, still not sure what to do.

"I can feel that rage, fresh and boiling under the surface. You're a very angry little girl," the demon said, smiling. "I'm not here to judge. That's the other guy's deal. I think you're justified in your anger. In fact, I have an offer for you."

Laura's eyes darted back and forth, looking for a weapon or some-thing she could use to defend herself. She spotted the knife, but it was well out of reach.

"I assure you, I haven't come to harm you. I've come to help," he offered, his face amused and somewhat quizzical. "That knife would do you no good anyway, even if you could get to it." The demon waved his hand, making a spectacle of turning the knife into a colorful scarf, snapping and turning it back again. "Silly mortal weapons are of no concern to me, child. If you must, you're welcome to pick it up and try stabbing me. It's amusing to me when people try."

"What... I wasn't..." she stammered, having been so easily pinned down. Flustered and afraid, she grimaced.

"Do not worry, child. I know what I look like. I know the effect I have on people. You're afraid. That wasn't my intent. Like I said, I'm here to help."

"Help with what?" Laura asked. "I don't need help from a mon-ster."

The demon folded a hand over his heart in mock hurt. "You wound me. I think we both know your monster is the man behind you. That red mark on your face is proof enough of that."

Laura's hand flew to the hot slap mark on her cheek, but she held firm. "Yes, well, monsters come in all shapes and sizes."

"You're far too young to be this cynical, but it is no matter. Let's get back to business. Are you interested in my offer?"

She paused a moment before replying, "I don't think you're supposed to enter into deals with the Devil, and you haven't even given me an offer to consider."

"Ah, but, my girl, you've already entered into an unholy covenant. Why else would I be here?" He smiled, showing a bright row of sharp teeth. "I assure you, this deal is much better than the one you've already agreed to. You really should pay attention when you're entering into contracts."

"Wha..."

"You accepted my gift, no?"

"What gift?" she asked, fairly certain she knew the answer, but not willing to admit it.

"You know very well what gift. You agreed to take it of your own free will, and you followed the terms my friend laid out. One devil's food cake per day. Correct?"

Laura's brain struggled to comprehend what the man was saying. They'd never met. She'd have remembered coming face to face with the Devil. Sure, she'd taken a gift from that crazy old woman, but that was something different. Wasn't it? She couldn't deny that she'd heard his voice before, drumming inside her head. So, in that way they were familiar.

The Devil watched with his amused smiling face as Laura worked things out in her head.

"It would have been a good idea to read the directions on those cake mix packets. No one ever does. The devil's in the details." The Devil clicked his tongue, a sound of disappointment, before moving on. "You'd have seen that ingesting each cake was draining your humanity, converting your form into something a little less...human. It was all very plainly printed below the ingredients list."

Crap.

Laura could feel the weighty horns protruding from both sides of her head. She ran her tongue across her teeth, noting the spikey fangs in her mouth. Somehow, the pain and the transformation were her fault, after all. Her mother told her not to rush growing up because she wouldn't like adult responsibilities, and Laura thought this was what her mother meant; not exactly, of course, but in essence.

"When you finished that last cake, you pledged your eternal soul to me, the Devil."

"All of this over an Easy-Bake Oven? You...you tricked me!" Laura's mind raced back to her exchange with the creepy old woman and he described it perfectly. She had done those things. Something else itched the back of her brain.

The marks.

Laura had thought the woman had nines on her arm, but now realized her mark was, in fact, *666*, the mark of the beast. She'd missed it and it was right there, staring her in the face.

"Now you're getting it," he said. "But I like you, and I want to offer you a choice, a new deal, if you will. I could take your soul right now, send you down to Hell to be a little worker bee. You're already mid-transformation, and I'm entitled to your soul. It's my right to collect, even though you failed to read the terms. But you've been more fun than anticipated, and I've got something better in mind for you."

Laura now knew her horns and teeth were real, that she hadn't hallucinated the whole thing, but it didn't bring her much comfort. However, she briefly entertained the notion that her father had smacked her hard enough to knock her out and that this was all some type of black-out hallucination. While that may have been the more logical conclusion, something told her this demon and his offer were real. Either way, she had no choice but to keep listening. There was no getting past him, and—she looked him up and down to assess his physique—no outrunning him. As her mom would say, "You run with the Devil, not away from him."

The beast looked at her, cocking his head side to side like a curious puppy. "I think you're special. So much rage for such a small girl. I think we can help each other out."

"How?" Laura asked, nervously shifting back and forth on her feet.

"Well, I will take your soul either way. It's mine. You're mine. That's unbreakable. But you'd be wasted down below running menial errands for some higher demon. I'd like you to help me punish the living. I'd like you to send wicked souls to Hell. Yes, that sounds lovely, an unsuspecting little girl doing the Devil's work. I love it." He laughed, a deep booming sound that rattled the flimsy trailer walls. "And I'd like you to start with him." The Devil pointed, once again, to Laura's father. "It's the perfect trial run."

"You want me to kill my father?" she asked, conflicted by the choice. "I can't do that. He's awful, but I'm not a murderer. I'm just an angry little girl."

The demon frowned her way. "Is he not a despicable man? Has he not hurt you? Surely, you had that knife in your hand for some reason. I may have pushed you to bring it, but the part where you pulled it out of that adorable vest of yours, that was all you."

"I mean, I had it in my hand and all, but that doesn't mean I want to be a killer. Blood and guts and gore are for movies, not my real life. Maybe I was just here to scare him, to get some payback or whatever. I'm not going to murder my own dad, no matter how awful he is." Laura crossed her arms, narrowing her eyes at the demon, standing her ground and making herself as large as possible.

The Devil scratched his chin, a thoughtful look on his face, before offering Laura a slightly amended option. "How's this? You don't have to pick up that knife and stab the man if you don't have the stomach for it. You just have to agree to let me take him, and I'll do the work from there."

He grabbed Laura's hand, opening her palm and pressing his nail into her flesh. Laura felt a small electric jolt pass from the demon into her. She pulled her hand away as quickly as possible, and inspected it to ensure she wasn't wounded. There was an ashy spot in the center of her palm, but no injury remained. "Nifty. What'd you just do?"

"I have given you all you need to complete the task I've set in front of you." The demon circled her, a hungry look in his eyes, and he continued, "You've got the power to send wicked souls straight to Hell simply by snapping your fingers."

"Okay, then..."

"Now, back to business. Give me the sinner standing in front of us. Agree to do this for me, and you'll be set free. You can go home to your mother. You can live your life. As long as you send me wicked souls, I will let you grow old and die. And when you come down below, there will be no suffering. No. You can join my legions. How's that sound? Instead of being dragged down to Hell right now to serve me, to suffer, you will be elevated to the status of demon upon your death. Gift me your father's eternal soul as a gesture of goodwill. You can choose the other souls all by yourself."

Laura considered the offer, the weight of the choice heavy in her chest. She wasn't equipped for such big decisions. She could barely settle on what to eat for dinner, let alone whether to give her father's soul to the Devil. This wasn't the choice for a child, and though she hated admitting it, she was still a child. Yet, it was a decision she had to make. There was no running, no hiding, and no breaking free. Was doing this the same as murder? She didn't think so, or maybe she just hoped not. She thought she could separate the two concepts because she wouldn't be hurting anyone and there wouldn't be any blood.

Laura closed her eyes and let the memories of her father's cruelty wash over her. Instead of cowering and running from them, she watched them on a reel inside her head. As the scenes rolled, each more violent than the next, she wept. Her father didn't deserve mercy. She didn't know if she was the right person to exact punishment for his misdeeds, but one thing was certain: he deserved it.

With her decision made, she opened her eyes, looked the Devil square in the face, and replied, "Yes, I'll do it." The anger inside of her body swelled, but instead of feeling pained or upset, she felt free. This was the only decision.

"Wonderful," the demon said, clapping with glee. "Now, let's unfreeze things and see how you do."

In a flash, her father lurched forward, grabbing at her neck. His hot hands began to squeeze. Laura pushed at him, attempting to free herself before remembering what the demon had said. She raised her left hand and snapped. Her father's grip went slack as a look of confusion registered on his face. His body pulsed red before exploding into a cloud of ash. Then he was no more.

"Delightful," the demon said.

At that moment, Laura's soul left her body. It was sucked from her skin all the way back to her bedroom and into the Easy-Bake Oven.

The toy oven vanished in a pop, landing back in the old woman's makeshift home, ready to capture a new young soul.

Laura's flesh ripped, tearing from her body, leaving her slimy and bleeding while also making way for her new dark green scales to grow in. She screamed as her flesh tore, opening like a fresh wound from head to toe. The white-hot pain consumed her as she fought to stay conscious during her transformation.

"Don't you look lovely," the Devil said, interested in her transformation. "No demon is the same, you know. Everyone looks so different. I never know what I'll get. This is my favorite part of the process." He looked on with a child-like glint of amusement on his face.

Laura's form was slick with sinew, and she looked on in repulsed wonder at her new demon skin. "I'm green and scaly. Is this permanent?"

"Yes, and also, no. You can see it if you want. But you can choose not to. Go ahead, try."

She closed her eyes, willing her body to look normal again. Not convinced it would work, she popped them open again and fawned over her now normal-looking hands and arms.

"Whoa." Reaching her hands up above her ears, she felt for the horns that had popped through a few days ago. There was no physical trace. She also ran her tongue over her teeth, noticing that they felt normal once again. "How did you make the horns and fangs go away?"

"I didn't. Not really. Think of yourself as a shape-shifter. If you imagine yourself green and scaled once again, those teeth and horns will return. You may, in fact, notice that all of your teeth come to little points. I can't say for sure because, like I said, each demon is unique."

"This is a lot to process."

"Lucky for you, you'll have plenty of time to think it through. I like the green better myself, but you can choose to see what you like. Others will see you as a normal little girl...unless they're wicked. Then they'll see the demon. It's a fun little trick to help you know which souls you can send my way. You don't have to send them all. I'll have them eventually. Just send the ones you want. There isn't a quota to meet, but if no souls show up, I'll come looking for you, and I won't be happy."

"Okay," she replied, still overwhelmed by the events unfolding in front of her.

"You've done well," the Devil said, patting Laura on her head. "It takes guts to send your own father to Hell."

"Thank you," she beamed, wanting nothing more than to please her new overlord.

"One more thing. You'll need the mark." He touched his hand behind her ear, emblazoning a tiny *666* on her skin. "That's better. I'll be off now. You have fun." The Devil turned and exited the trailer before walking out into the world and fading from view.

Laura rubbed at the burning sensation behind her ear, fumbling to trace the *666*.

"Well, crap."

Chapter 11

LAURA STOOD, STILL SOMEWHAT shocked about what had just transpired. Was this real life? Or was she trapped in a dream? She didn't know if she could tell the difference anymore.

What was that thing Dr. Yardley told me to do during my dreams? Oh, reality testing!

Laura opened her palm and inspected it. It looked normal enough. Taking the fingers from her right hand, she attempted to poke the open left palm. Her fingers didn't pass through.

Okay, probably real life.

Let's do one more.

This time, she pinched her nose and tried to breathe. She couldn't. In her dreams, she could always breathe.

Double crap.

"This is really happening then," she said, wanting some noise to fill the suddenly empty space. Her father was ding-dong dead. He couldn't hurt her anymore. He couldn't hurt her mother. She liked that part, but feared having to face him in the underworld.

The demon said I wouldn't suffer down below. Maybe I'll never have to see my father again.

She hated to think it, but the Devil seemed reasonable; he liked Laura. So, maybe he'd grant her a kindness later on.

"What the hell am I thinking? Ha. Hell." The entire situation was unbelievable. "I'm going to have to think about the last few days for a very long time for any of it to make sense."

She didn't feel bad for snapping her fingers and sending her wretched father to Hell. She thought she should have felt bad because even though he was a terrible person, he was still a person, her father, nonetheless. But she felt only relief, and if she dug a little, some joy as well. Needing a minute to think everything through, she stepped forward and sat in her father's aged swivel chair.

Laura looked at the hands of her human form while examining her inner thoughts. Her soul was forfeit to the Devil, and she had lost it in those moments of transformation. She felt a piece of herself break off and float away. Still, she felt the full range of human emotions. She wanted to be good, wanted to make her mother proud. She'd assumed losing her soul would taint her, turn her evil, but it hadn't. If anything, she simply felt free.

"And so, I'm a what? A demon now? Is that even a thing?"

But she knew it was. She'd felt it, the transformation, the Devil's gifts coursing through her veins. She closed her eyes and imagined seeing her slick, green-scaled skin. When she opened them, it was there, a thick, shell-like green armor glistening in the dim light.

Laura's heart began to race as things finally hit her. Her breaths came in hard, quick bursts as she shuddered there in her dead father's chair. She sat, zoned out, and stared at the wall for what could have been minutes or hours, soaking in her new station in life and wondering how she would manage to be a child, go to school, and reap evil souls for Satan.

The ringing of the office telephone jolted her back to reality.

"Crap," she exclaimed, noticing the clock on the wall read 4:00. Her mother would be home in an hour, give or take, and she needed to beat her there. Not wanting to chance being seen or crossing paths with her mom, she had no choice but to take the long way back and hope that time was on her side.

As she left the trailer, wiping the door handles off as she went, she crossed paths with Skimbleshanks one more time. "Oh no, boy. I can't leave you here, can I?"

The dog whimpered in her general direction. She went around to where he was tethered and unclipped the line from its anchor. Not seeing a leash nearby, she wound the cord around her arm several times and tugged on it to let Skimbleshanks know it was time to go. "You're gonna come back home with me, okay? Mom's not going to be happy, but I can't very well leave you all alone here."

The dog eyed her warily before falling into step behind her. "It's okay, boy. I'll take good care of you. This place sucks anyway. You'll like it at home much better."

As they walked, Skimbleshanks relaxed. He seemed to recognize her instead of just fearing her. She knew dogs could perceive things, and she assumed Skimbleshanks knew there was something wrong with her. But she would win him over again. The bigger issue was her mother. How could she just bring home Dad's junkyard dog without arousing suspicion? Thankfully, she had the longer walk home to devise a plan, which, even though she was hurrying, was enough time to think up something convincing.

Instead of bringing Skimbleshanks in and having to concoct some nonsense story, she'd leave him out front, tied to the black walnut tree in her front yard. She could feign ignorance that way, and she knew her softhearted mother would take the dog in, at least for the time being.

As Laura walked, she crossed paths with several passersby, none of whom paid her any attention.

Deep breaths.

See, you look normal. Everything is fine.

Moving on, she caught a young man in a knit cap staring at her in creepy silence. She paused, turning her head to look him directly in the eyes, and he shuffled backward, a look of fear pressed into his disturbed face. Laura looked at her hand for a moment before smiling at the man and snapping. For a sliver of a second, he looked shocked before bursting into a cloud of ash just as her father had done.

Easy, peasy. I can do this.

Briefly, she wondered what the man had done wrong. He could see her new face. So, it might have been something fairly awful. Not knowing felt a little wrong. Next time she'd need to get at least a name so she could investigate the person online or something.

The clock rounded 4:30, and Laura hustled the last few blocks home. Mrs. Roth was, thankfully, nowhere to be seen. She didn't see anyone else outside when she got to her house. So, she made quick work of looping Skimbleshanks' tether to the tree.

"Be a good boy and lie down, okay?" The dog relented and, though confused, seemed happy enough to rest in the cool grass for now. Laura rushed inside, ran upstairs to change into loungewear, and jumped into bed with a book. The clock read 4:50.

Made it.

A few minutes later, Laura heard the distinct jingle of keys as her mom came in through the garage. "Laura?" she called, sounding slightly concerned. "Laura, are you up there?"

Okay. You can do this.

Stay calm. Be normal.

She doesn't know. She can't know.

Laura hopped out of bed and shuffled her way into the hall, purposely moving a little slower than normal. "Mom? Are you home already?"

"Oh, thank goodness. I've been worried. I need you to come downstairs."

Taking it slow, Laura made her way across the hall before descending the stairs.

This is fine. Everything will be fine.

As she rounded the corner, spying her mother, she made sure to open her eyes wide in feigned shock as she noticed her mom standing at the landing, looking frantic, and holding Skimbleshanks by his tether. "Uh, Mom? What's going on?"

Her mother looked at her, studying her face, seemingly worried and suspicious. "I don't know, Laura. I was hoping you could tell me!"

"Why? Wait...what? Tell you what?"

Her mother tapped her foot impatiently on the tile floor. "Well, for starters, Mrs. Roth called and told me you were stumbling around outside like some kind of drunk."

Laura laughed deeply and well. "She what? Mom. I would never! Do I look drunk to you?"

"You do not," she agreed. "Why would Mrs. Roth call me with such a wild story then? What did you do?"

Laura tried to look hurt. "What? Mom, I don't know what you're talking about? And..." she pointed at Skimbleshanks, "why do you have Dad's dog?"

"I don't know, Laura. We'll get to this creature after we finish our talk. So, you're saying you weren't drinking, and you didn't do anything today?"

"I mean, I did stuff, but I wasn't wandering around outside like a drunk jerk. I'm not Dad."

Her mother looked pained. "Were you outside at all? Did you see Mrs. Roth today?"

"No," Laura began in earnest. "Wait, yes! But, also, no." She crossed her arms in front of her in an annoyed pout. "Let me start over. You've got me all confused. Yes, I went outside earlier, just for a minute, to check the mail. Then I skipped back inside. Literally, I skipped, if that's important. No, I did not see the neighbor lady."

"Hmmm..." Laura's mother thought on it for a minute, and while she didn't seem completely satisfied, she dropped the issue. "And you didn't see your father today?"

"No, I haven't seen that jerk for months."

"Language, Laura!"

"What? Jerk isn't a real swear, and he is a jerk. So..."

"You're not wrong," her mother replied, "but where did this beast of a dog come from?"

Laura shrugged before crossing the room and falling to her knees in front of Skimbleshanks. She scratched him behind the ears and told him he was a good boy. "So, are we keeping him?"

"I don't know, Laura. I'll call the junkyard and see what your father has to say."

It was near imperceptible, but Laura noticed her mother shudder at the thought of speaking to the man who'd beat her mentally and physically. At that moment, Laura was certain she'd made the right decision. Her father was a monster. He deserved to be punished by other monsters for all eternity.

Laura unclipped Skimbleshanks, "Come on, boy. Follow me!" The dog tentatively followed Laura to the kitchen, where he was treated to a full slice of cheddar cheese and a bowl of water. They didn't have dog bowls, so Laura filled a cereal bowl and placed it on the floor for the dog. "There ya go, bud. We'll treat you real good."

After seeing to the dog, Laura peeked back into the living room. She spotted her mom with her head in her hands. She wasn't crying, but she seemed stressed. After a few moments, she took out her cell and called the junkyard. No one answered, so she left a short message. "Kevin. Why was your dog tied to a tree in front of my house? You know you're not supposed to violate the restraining order. What do you want me to do with Skimbleshanks?"

After that, her mother called her lawyer and then made a police report just to be safe.

Laura and her mom sat together at the kitchen table, eating beef Stroganoff. Skimbleshanks got his own plate as well.

"Can we keep him, Mom?" Laura asked. "He's such a good boy."

"I don't know, kiddo. We'll see what happens. For now, he can stay. If the police want him or your father demands we return him, I don't know. This feels like a trick. Let's not talk about it anymore, okay?"

Laura's mother looked haunted, her face a little more gaunt than usual, a hint of darkness under each eye. Her stress was apparent. So Laura nodded.

"Tell me more about your day. Did you solve the horn problem?"

Laura chuckled. "Sorry about that, Mom. I just wanted a day off. I needed a break from life."

"I get it, kid. We all need a mental health day every now and again. Next time, just ask. Skip the horns and fangs routine."

Laura gave a half-hearted laugh. "Deal."

Chapter 12

6 weeks, 6 days, and 6 minutes later.

LAURA SETTLED INTO HER new routine, slipping in and out of her demon disguise at will and sending souls to the Devil. She was surprised at how many wicked people she came across in her small town. She didn't go far and didn't vary much in routine, but wayward souls seemed to cross her path almost daily. She didn't snap at all of them, like Mr. Fritz, the man from the insurance office a few doors from her mother's shop. She didn't know what he'd done wrong—she almost never knew—but it didn't feel right to send a neighbor to Hell. She laughed when he dropped his coffee and ran screaming down the road the other day. It was funny every time, and probably her favorite part of the new position. She hoped he'd run straight to some church to repent so she never had to send him to Hell. Though, she wasn't entirely certain repenting worked. No one had given her a rule book.

The Devil had allowed her some wiggle room and she decided to take it, for now. She wasn't the only one reaping souls, of that she was sure. So, if someone else got Mr. Fritz, she wouldn't have to think about it, wouldn't have to lie to her mother when she brought up the subject. Being open and honest with her mother was still very much important to her. Sure, she couldn't share everything with Mom anymore, but she wanted to maximize what she could share.

Her father's disappearance, while for the best, was a hard thing for Laura to lie about. She wanted to tell her mother what had happened, wanted her mom to feel safe, but she couldn't. She also wasn't sure whether her mother would view her as a savior or a killer, and she didn't want to roll those dice. So, she fibbed to her mom and lied to the police when they came sniffing around. Only Skimbleshanks had any inkling of what'd happened, but he couldn't tell anyone.

His situation had certainly improved. Her mother fed him high-end filler-free foods, twice a day, and he got all the pets his little dog heart could want. It was a far cry from being chained up in that rusty yard with only a drunkard to look after him. Even if he could give Laura's secrets away, she didn't think he would. They'd come to an understanding.

Her father's case still hadn't closed, but life started feeling better and her mother seemed less on edge than before, which brought a smile to Laura's face. For a while, police visits and calls were the norm, but as the trail went cold, those tapered off. There was no sign of her father. He was simply there one day and gone the next. Despite a small protest from her mother, they'd kept the dog and settled into a new routine as a trio.

"Kid, are you ready for school?" her mom called up to her, an urgent tone in her voice.

"Yeah, yeah, yeah. I'm on my way." Laura flew down the stairs in a blur of disheveled clothing and frizzy hair before grabbing the Pop-Tart from her mother's hand. "Thanks for thinking of me, Mom."

"I know your ways. If I don't have one of these in hand, who knows if you'd ever eat breakfast."

"Who, indeed?" Laura replied, winking at her mom.

Hopping in the car, Laura noticed two empty Starbucks cups in the center console and eyed her mother suspiciously. She certainly hadn't enjoyed a delicious Starbucks beverage, which either meant her mom had developed a caffeine problem or someone else had been in the car. "Hmmm..."

"What are you hmmm-ing about over there?"

"Oh, nothing. Wanna turn on some sweet jams? Extra loud?"

"You know it," her mom replied, cranking the volume to 20 and pressing play on David Bowie's "Life on Mars." Together they belted the lyrics on the short drive to school before Laura hopped out, waved goodbye to her mother, and sauntered into school.

School improved tenfold since Laura's little change was over. She'd always enjoyed most of it, save for math class. Mrs. Sharp was a stealer of joy, and a very wicked person. She tried to hide it, and Laura assumed the booze helped, but Laura could tell Mrs. Sharp saw her green, scaly demon self.

She flinched away from Laura, walked around her in the classroom, leaving a wide berth between them, and the bullying had ceased. Truly, this improved everyone's experience. But the rat-faced woman still came in red-eyed and slurring. She didn't teach them much of anything, which would leave the entire class behind and failing at the end of the year. It was unfair.

Laura leaned over, whispering to her neighbor Dominic, "You understanding any of this?"

"Why bother?" he asked, turning his attention back to scratching some message on the top of his wooden desk.

"Yeah, I guess so." Laura narrowed her eyes, watching Mrs. Sharp bump the corner of her desk and mutter something under her breath. While she didn't want to poof the woman away, she felt like she could do something. Though, the thought of Mrs. Sharp blowing up into a cloud of dust and then settling slowly into the industrial carpet right in front of everyone's eyes brought Laura a certain degree of joy. Ta-da.

Discreetly, she pulled the cell phone out of her pocket. Several other students were tapping away under their desks or scrolling across social media feeds. Mrs. Sharp wasn't sober enough to notice today. Laura opened the record app and pressed the button to begin recording before tucking the phone mostly into her tank top and pulling her zip-up hoodie close around her. The phone was camouflaged enough that her teacher wouldn't see it. If she did, she'd maybe see two or three phones.

"Okay, kidssss, Mrs. Sharp'sss gonna have a wittle rest here. Take out your boo...boo..." She laughed at a joke no one else seemed to understand. "Take out your bookssss and solve problems or some-thing." With that, Mrs. Sharp hiccupped. Her head bobbed forward as she drifted off to sleep, saliva dripping down from the corner of her half-closed mouth.

"That'll do," Laura said, before pulling the phone out, stopping the video, and trimming a few seconds from the start and end to better hide her identity.

Some of her classmates looked up, laughing at the teacher before returning to their scrolling or doodling. A few braver kids crept to the front of the room to take selfies with Mrs. Sharp. What they planned to do with them, Laura didn't know. She hoped they'd post to their various social media accounts to help support what she was about to do. The more evidence they had, the better this would work. While Mrs. Sharp was often sloppy, she'd escalated in the presence of a literal demon, and that was working to everyone's advantage.

With everyone preoccupied, Laura created a fake email and YouTube account where she uploaded her footage of Mrs. Sharp, making sure to email the link to her principal before deleting the email address entirely. She realized it could probably be traced back to her, but she'd done nothing wrong. So if someone did want to find her, she wasn't terribly worried. She wasn't sure what would happen to Mrs. Sharp. Would she be disciplined? Let go? Barred from ever teaching again? Regardless, Laura hoped it'd improve the situation of her classmates. In her opinion, Mrs. Sharp had to go.

After leaving class, the rest of her day was uneventful. She spoke with a few other children, preferring not to make close friends but also not wanting to completely alienate herself. Her mother picked her up, and they spent the afternoon together at the shop before grabbing fast food and heading home for the evening. Laura noted that the two coffee cups had been cleaned up since the morning, but she didn't bring it up.

After school the next day, Laura hopped into her mother's car with a satisfied smile on her face.

"And what's got you all glowy? You're not usually this chipper. Is it a boy? Please tell me it's a boy...or, um, girl. Either way."

Laura scrunched up her face in mock disgust. "Ew, Mom. No thanks."

Her mom gave a short laugh before pressing the issue a little further. "Well, what is it then? Spill."

"You'll never guess what happened today!" Laura's eyes were wide with excitement.

"Obviously. That's why I'm asking."

"Ha. Ha. Funny, Mom. Okay, so, Mrs. Sharp was not in school today."

"Ah, old rat-face is out sick. I bet that did make your day." Her mom turned the key in the ignition, starting the car, and backed out of the parking stall to drive home. "I can see why you're so upbeat this afternoon."

"No! No, that's not it at all."

Raising an eyebrow, but keeping her attention on the road, her mother replied, "Go on..."

"She. Was. Fired."

"Whoa. Happy day to you! Are you sure?"

"Yessssss! The vice principal was our sub today. He apologized for Mrs. Sharp's misconduct." Laura paused to tip a fake bottle into her mouth. "You know, glug, glug."

"Laura, that's inappropriate. Was your teacher drinking at work?"

"She certainly stumbled around and slurred enough."

Looking stern for a moment, her mother glanced her way briefly. "You should have told me about that."

"No one believes kids. What was I gonna say, 'Guess what, Mom? My awful rodent of a teacher is a drunkard'?"

"Hmmm... Alright, we can table that part. How do you know that's what happened?"

"Well, they brought in a, I don't know, grief counselor? And they said if we needed to talk about our experiences in the classroom or about substance abuse, the counselor would be in a little office for the next month."

"That's good, or concerning, or maybe both."

"Ding. Dong. The witch is gone!"

Her mother patted her on the leg. "I'm glad you're happy, dear. Now for the bad news: it's your turn to poop scoop the yard this weekend."

"Yuuucckkkk. Why you gotta bring me down, Mom?"

They both laughed.

"ELO, nice. I've taught you well. Go ahead and call me Bruce," her mother said before turning up the classic rock station.

"Funny, Mom. It's a good thing I'm well versed in old person music or I wouldn't get your lame joke."

"Old? You better take that back! I'm the portrait of youth and beauty."

"Okay then. You're young and whatever." Laura gave another hearty laugh after the exchange.

They both, mother and daughter, bopped along to the music until coming to a stop at What's Sewing On.

Laura hopped out, asking if she could wander down the block for some snacks.

"Homework first, then snacks."

"Ugh, fine, Mom. Way to ruin my high."

Chapter 13

'When Laura's mother finally brought Garret home, she was ready. While her mother had kept the dating from her, she knew. There'd be the occasional extra cup in the car or at the kitchen table. Neither of them mentioned it. The cups were eventually cleared away and they went on with their usual routine.

Other things had changed, and Laura couldn't help but think it had all been due to the disappearance of her father. It finally allowed her mom to relax and move forward. While she wasn't eager to share her mother with a new person, she knew it was inevitable and certainly didn't want her to grow old alone. Her mother's Talbots suits were replaced with jeans and band t-shirts more often than not. She'd often throw a fitted blazer over the top in more professional settings. This was the mother Laura knew she'd always been meant to be, as cool on the outside as she was inside.

"Laura, can you come downstairs for a minute? There's someone I'd like you to meet."

This was it, the moment of truth. "I'll be down in a few, Mom. Just changing." Laura crept to the top of the stairs and peered down at the man below. He was of average height and build, had short side-parted brown hair, and a bushy mustache. Laura had expected someone cooler and edgier, not some middle-aged dork with a lampshade mustache. Regardless of Laura's assessment of his physical appearance, the only thing that really mattered was the reaction he had once she stepped into the room.

If he recoiled or screamed, Laura had resolved to poof him on the spot and come clean to her mother. The secrets weighed on her, and there was no real opportunity to work the whole demon soul-reaper thing into normal conversation. Her mom hadn't believed her about the fangs and horns. She certainly wouldn't believe her now, not without proof. Still, that terrified Laura. She wasn't sure if her mother would react in horror, if she'd be traumatized by the incident, or if she'd be able to wrap her mind around it and thank Laura for protecting her again.

"Kid, hurry up, would ya? We don't have all day, you know?" her mom called up again, sounding slightly irked.

"Yeah, yeah, yeah," she responded while noisily bounding down the stairs.

As she stepped into view, she noticed the man was slightly uncomfortable, shuffling back and forth on his feet. But he didn't have any kind of visceral reaction to her appearance. Laura wasn't sure if she was relieved or disappointed.

"Laura, I'd like you to meet my friend, Garret." She smiled awkwardly, looking between her daughter and new boyfriend.

"Friend?" Laura replied, a small upward inflection at the end of her question.

The man smiled nervously and held out a hand. Laura looked at it before extending her own and grasping the hand firmly in what felt like an awkwardly professional gesture. Instead of speaking directly to Garret, she looked at her mother. "Garret here must really enjoy coffee."

Laura took her hand back and placed it neatly at her side while her mother blushed in realization.

"You knew, didn't you?"

"Yeah, Mom. Of course, I knew. Look at you! You're a whole new person. Can we burn those old suits?"

"Laura, that's not appropriate."

"They're pretty ugly. It's a compliment. I'm saying you look good, happy even."

"I see," her mother responded, biting her lip, and not sure where to take the conversation.

Garret cleared his throat before joining in. "Well, you weren't lying about this one. She's a bit precocious, isn't she?"

"I'm not sure what that word means, Mom's new *friend* Garret, but if you hurt her, I'll have to kill you."

"Uh...and protective, it seems," Garret finished.

"Laura, please do not threaten people when I bring them into our home." Her mother winked at her. "But thanks for looking out."

Introductions complete, Laura excused herself before leaving the two adults in the living room to do whatever gross romantic things they had planned.

As Laura returned to her room, it was filled with the unpleasant scent of rotten eggs, a stench that made her retch. She looked around cautiously, uncertain of what terrible thing she'd encounter. The door closed behind her and the red Devil stepped out from where the door had previously been.

"Ugh, you again?" She huffed.

"Do not disrespect me, child. I like you, but if you cross the line, you won't like my retaliation."

"Okay, but why are you here? I thought we'd concluded our deal?" She crossed her arms, her patience thin.

"There has been a complication," he began, pausing for dramatic effect, "with your father."

That got Laura's attention. She jumped from slightly annoyed to fully anxious, fearful, and stressed in equal amounts. "What kind of complication?"

"He is not obedient."

"Is that all? I could have told you that! He's the worst."

"Yes, but this goes beyond what's normal. Usually, we can break the spirits of pride-filled men. However, despite trying all of our best tortures, your father has stood defiant. He wants only revenge for what you've done to him. While he's soulless, like all of the damned, this is a level we don't particularly like dealing with."

In confusion, she replied, "Isn't that, like, the whole deal with Hell? You're all soulless little monsters wreaking havoc on things?"

The Devil nodded, scratching his chin in contemplation. "That is part of the equation, yes. But we have rules and boundaries. Look at you. You are soulless, yes? Has that changed you?"

"Only a little, I guess."

"Exactly. The soul isn't a be-all end-all. I like to collect them. They're pretty. But you remain who you were when you had one. So, Hell isn't full of monsters, not like you think. It is a society where the damned go to be punished for their misdeeds. My demons carry out those punishments, much like you're doing for me now. It is their job. They are...employees."

Laura had never thought of Hell in terms of corporate life, but from what she knew, she could see the similarities. People hated the greedy corporate machine. "I don't see what any of this has to do with me."

"Ah," he replied, crossing the room to sit on her bed. He patted the spot beside him. "Come sit."

"This must be serious." She walked closer to the demon and sat beside him, like it was the most normal thing in the world.

"When a being like your father comes along, we destroy it."

Confused again, she nodded for him to continue.

"Everything he is, was, ever would be, ceases to exist. It is a true final death. Very few experience this fate. It is incredibly painful, and then there's nothing."

"Are you here for my permission or something?" She looked the Devil in his eyes. "If that's what you want, you have it. I don't ever want to see the man again."

"Not quite... I want you to do it."

"What part of 'never want to see the man again' did you not understand?"

"You realize I am the dark lord, yes?"

She nodded.

"Good, let me explain. This is important. Consider it a final test, your declaration to me, the Devil. Sending someone to their final end is never to be taken lightly, and I want you to be the one to do it."

"What do I get in exchange?"

"Nothing, Laura. I've given all I will give."

"Do I have a choice?"

"No."

"Great. What do I have to do?"

The Devil explained the process was as simple as a snap of her fingers. She had the power already, but could only use it down below, a place she'd yet to visit. While she'd spend her retirement in Hell, she hadn't planned to see it until she died. Nodding solemnly in understanding, she agreed to travel to Hell for this one task.

"I don't want to be a murderer," she said, pointing out what she had when the Devil first offered her a new deal. "You know that. That's like the whole premise of my deal."

"This isn't killing, per se, as he is most assuredly already dead."

At war with herself, Laura let his words wash over her. As she contemplated, the Devil used his sharp talon to draw a line in the floor, revealing a fiery pit which led down into the underbelly of Hell.

"What am I supposed to do with that?"

"Jump in," he said, laughing, that great booming sound filling Laura's ears like it had when she was going through her transformation.

Looking down into the pit, Laura gave a shrug and jumped in. She fell through the fire-lined portal, admiring the yellows and oranges licking the sides of the tunnel. Were she not headed to Hell to give her father a final death, she'd have thought the view was beautiful, magical even. Trying to count, but unable to focus, Laura wasn't sure how long she fell, only that she landed softly in what looked like a dimly lit mine. Screams filled the air.

"Those are the damned, screaming for release. Do you like it?"

"I think you know I don't."

"Suit yourself," the Devil said. "Your father is straight through there." He pointed to an iron-barred gate. "Follow me."

Laura tentatively crossed the corridor, slowly creeping closer to her father. Her hands were shaking, fear coursing through her veins. Never having expected to see him again, she was less than thrilled at a potential face-off. She could see him, crouched in the corner of the small room behind the barred door. The sound of her shuffling caused his head to snap in her direction, and upon seeing her he flew forward, reaching his arms through the bars of the door and trying to grab at her frail, childlike form. She thought he'd been terrifying in life, but in death his eyes were wild and hate-filled, a red glow amplifying the degree to which he was rage-filled.

Great gobs of spit flew from his mouth as he screamed out, "You little bitch!"

Laura backed up, bumping into the demon behind her as she went. The Devil put a large hand on her shoulder, steadying the girl, and looked her in the eyes. "You can do this."

She nodded back at the Devil as a single tear rolled down her face before turning back to the monster in the locked room.

Her father wore his signature indignant sneer, and he laughed haughtily before addressing her once again. "Who do you think you are? You're nothing. You wouldn't even be here without me. I made you. What right do you have to banish me to this terrible place? I should have throttled you, strangled the life from your gangly body so that no one would ever have to love you. I should have done it to your mother before you came along. A daughter should respect her father. I deserve that much." With that, he pressed his face up against the bars and spit directly in her face.

Laura filled with the uncomfortable rage that she knew all too well. The only thing ever to bring out that type of anger in the girl was the man standing directly in front of her. She wasn't sure he was a man anymore. In fact, she wasn't convinced he ever was. If so, he was the most pathetic excuse for a man she'd ever met.

She wiped his rancid spittle from her face, shaking her hand and splashing the strings of saliva back down to the ground, before standing with her head held high and replying, "I don't think you understand what's going on here, Father. You are not in control anymore. You can't hurt me. You can't hurt Mom."

"Little girl, you think that just because I'm locked here in this room I can't hurt you? You'll be having screaming nightmares of me until the day you die."

Laura carefully considered his words, pausing to puzzle out the last time she'd had a nightmare. She smiled in delight. They'd stopped the day she sent him to Hell.

"Why are you smiling?"

Laura looked at him, all the fear she felt in her bedroom melting away in that moment. "I used to fear you, but I don't anymore. You don't mean anything to me. You don't mean anything to Mom. You certainly don't mean anything to her new boyfriend. She's happy now. We are happy now. And do you know what my favorite part is?"

"What's that? Blah. Blah. Blah," he said, voice still thick with condescension.

"You're so awful that Hell doesn't even want you. This is where they send all the bad guys, and no one here, none of the demons, wants to see your face. How epic is it that you're this terrible?"

Her father sputtered, unable to find the words for a witty retort.

"And guess what, Dad? I'm the one who gets to send you into nothingness. All I have to do is snap my little fingers and you'll die a final death screaming in agony."

"What?" he sputtered. "What? No! No, no, no! You can't—"

"I think that's about enough from you," Laura said. "Goodbye forever."

With that, she smiled warmly in his general direction before snapping her fingers. His body lit in white-hot flames and his skin charred, smoking, and stinking up the chamber. He screamed the pathetic screams of a dying animal until the burning had eaten his lungs away. She watched as his skin dripped to the floor, forming a mass of gray, lumpy goo. She stood waiting in companionable silence next to the Devil as the flames eventually extinguished. In the aftermath, no trace of her father or any remains existed. Looking up at the demon next to her, she broke out into full guffawing laughter, the noisy, ugly kind. She laughed and laughed and laughed until her belly ached.

Finally, she looked up at the Devil and said, "I really am a demon, aren't I?"

He looked down at her, smiling in the way she'd always wanted her father to. "Yes, Laura. That you are. You've done well. Let's get you back home."

Epilogue
66 years and six minutes later

AN OLD WOMAN NOW, Laura was weary of her mortal life. She'd spent years living a normal human existence. She grew up, married the woman of her dreams, and settled down with three cats. Of course, it was difficult to hide her side hustle of reaping souls for the Devil, but she felt as if she'd done the world a great service, eliminating so much evil from the planet.

She stood, joints creaking in protest, and hobbled over to her oven. After turning it on to pre-heat, she sat to enjoy an ice-cold glass of tea. The air around her crackled, causing the remaining white hairs on her arms to stand on end.

"Hello, demon. It's nice of you to pop by."

"You're looking world weary, Laura, and your souls have slowed to a trickle."

"I'm not as limber as I once was." She laughed at her comical understatement. "Why don't you come and sit a while with me."

The Devil nodded, pulling out the chair across from her and having a seat. Laura reached out to clasp his hands, letting her human form slip. She knew he preferred the demon.

"Isn't this nice?" she asked. The oven beeped, indicating it had reached the desired temperature. "Excuse me a moment. I need to put something in the oven."

Laura wandered to the kitchen, leaving the Devil to sip tea at the table.

Once her family had all died, including her mother and dopey stepfather, Garret, and her friends had grown old and forgetful, Laura felt it was time to shuffle off her mortal coil and finally join her friend, the Devil, in Hell, where a new life and a new eternal adventure awaited her. She was glad to see her last remaining friend again. They sat together chatting about how life had changed on Earth, and the Devil regaled her with stories of bawdy demons and wayward souls. When the oven dinged a second time, she stood and shuffled to the kitchen.

Laura returned a few moments later with two plates. Each had a thick slab of warm devil's food cake. She placed one in front of her friend before sitting with the remaining plate. "I thought we could share a treat, you and I."

The Devil chuckled, his deep voice filling her modest dining room. "Devil's food. It's good to see you haven't lost your sense of humor."

They ate in companionable silence. Once finished, Laura spoke. "I think I'm ready to go with you."

"I thought you might be. Your eternal body will be much more comfortable. Shall we?" he asked, grabbing her by the hand and leading her back down into Hell where she'd live on, wreaking havoc on men like her father, dancing in their blood, drinking up their essence, and giggling as she went about her job, a favorite of her lord and master.

Three cakes were all it took, three cakes to damnation, an unholy covenant made by imbibing mediocre cakes made in a damned children's toy.

Three hundred miles south, a bedraggled woman sat on a street corner, screaming obscenities at innocent passersby, with a well-worn trash bag at her side, waiting for the next ripe child to waltz by. She ran her knobby fingers over the *666* she'd carved into her arm so long ago and smiled, thinking back to all the good work she'd done for her lord and savior, the Devil himself.

Acknowledgements

Three years ago, I saw a post from Hailey Piper about how she challenged herself to publish 100 things in five years. I decided to follow in those footsteps and push myself to get writing again. I'm currently in year four and just rounded the 70 publication mark. It was the kick I needed to jump back into creating. I'm set on hitting that goal of 100 publications in the next year and a half. I want to thank Hailey and her spirit for helping me get back on track. I'd also like to thank the community of writers I've met on this journey, especially my Pink Shock Coven sisters, Lylith Nix, Greta T. Bates, and E.H Regan for their support and their creative voices.

About the Author

Jessica Gleason finds writing horror therapeutic. So, she puts her nightmares on paper for your enjoyment. She often draws from her AAPI culture and lived experience to bring occult-flavored horror to life. Her daytime persona is a college professor in the American Midwest. Jessica's recent releases include *Playing Hooky* (Unnerving Books), *The Dangerous Miss Ventriloquist* (Evil Cookie Publishing), *Madison Murphy* (Cupid's Arrow Publishing), and *Damned Before Daylight* (Cupid's Arrow Publishing). Follow her on Instagram or Threads (@j.g.writes), where she hosts the #WeWriteHorror challenge.

www.ingramcontent.com/pod-product-compliance
Lightning Source LLC
Chambersburg PA
CBHW030942310726
48969CB00008B/2345